A distinguished academic, Luiz Alfredo Garcia-Roza is a bestselling novelist who lives in Rio de Janeiro. The Espinosa mysteries have been translated into five languages. This is the sixth book in the series.

Also by Luiz Alfredo Garcia-Roza

Blackout

Blackout

An Inspector Espinosa Mystery

Luiz Alfredo

GARCIA-ROZA

Translated by Benjamin Moser

Picador

Henry Holt and Company
New York

ISBN-13: 978-0-312-42886-0
ISBN-10: 0-312-42886-3

Originally published in Brazil in 2006 under the title *Espinosa Sem
Saida* by Companhia das Letras, São Paulo

First published in the United States by Henry Holt and Company

First Picador Edition: July 2009

10 9 8 7 6 5 4 3 2 1

Blackout

PART I

It was early afternoon, the hottest hour of the day, when the water in the faucet was warm, the asphalt on the streets sizzling, and the cloudless sky unperturbed by the slightest breeze.

The boy was sitting on the stairs in front of the house with his feet on the sidewalk, his elbows resting on his knees, and his chin leaning into his hands. He must have been around seven or eight, and was wearing shorts, a T-shirt, and sandals. He was looking around slowly, his brown eyes examining the ground, as though he was just checking out the sidewalk because it happened to be in the direction his head was pointing. He looked like he was waiting for something he knew would take a long time to arrive.

He knew all the houses on the street, and had been inside a few of them. They all resembled his own: two stories, a garden in the front and a yard behind. Looking at the street he knew every tree, every crack in the sidewalk, every secret entrance in the walls between the houses, every car parked along the curb; he knew the ice-cream man, the postman, the delivery boys; he knew the dogs that were wandering down the sidewalks and the ones that, at that time of day, were nowhere to be seen. From his vantage point on the stoop, the boy watched that little private world, which, though limited in space, was infinitely detailed, filled with secrets, hiding places, inhabitants small and large, mysteries.

The shadows were so strong and clear that they seemed to be painted onto the ground. There was no sign of any wildlife. If any bird ventured to fly, it was to seek protection within the branches of a tree. And when the odd car drove by, the contact of the tires with the asphalt produced a sticky noise.

From the window on the second floor, the man had been looking out for some time at the boy sitting at the gate. He thought about telling him to get out of the sun, to go find somewhere in the shade, to protect himself, but at that distance the man would have to shout and he was worried about disturbing the peace. He didn't know if his cry would, in fact, disturb anyone, or even if it was possible to disturb anything there. There was nobody else on the street; there didn't seem to be anyone inside the houses, not even inside the boy's house: the shutters were closed and there was clearly no movement outside it. Maybe everybody was asleep. The boy was alone at the gate.

The man pretended to leave the window, but he kept looking out at the street. Making up his mind, he took up his original position, leaning with his arms on the windowsill. He fixed his gaze on the boy as obstinately as the boy looked at the sidewalk in front of his gate, but not with the same calm. The boy didn't show any sign of discomfort or suffering. The sun and the heat didn't seem to affect him, and he gave the impression that he would do the same thing if it were raining. The man may have thought that boys are always doing something. At least that's how he had been. Even when they are alone, boys play with little cars, marbles, stones, imaginary friends. But that boy wasn't playing, or even moving. He was just looking.

From the window, the man saw the other three turn the corner onto the same sidewalk, coming toward the boy. He also noticed when the boy saw them coming and turned his head slightly toward the right. Of the three, one was much bigger, maybe as old as thirteen; the other two were about the same size as the boy, though they seemed to be older. They were shoeless and shirtless. Like the boy, they were all wearing shorts, though the two smaller boys were wearing dirtier, threadbare versions. The boy moved his head back to its original position and kept looking at the sidewalk in front of him. The three approached lazily, walking slowly and jauntily, talking among themselves, their eyes on the gate.

From where he was, the man couldn't see all the details, and couldn't make out what they were talking about. The new arrivals were poor kids, and the box of food they were passing around under the direction of the oldest was further proof of that. The man watched as the three arrived at the point of the sidewalk where the boy was and sat down on the curb, their backs facing him. The boy kept his elbows pressed into his knees, his head in his hands, and his eyes trained on the sidewalk, except now the three strangers had entered his field of vision.

As soon as they sat on the curb, the three resumed the lunch rotation. There was only one container of food. The oldest boy served himself, taking out a little handful, two or three times in a row; then he passed the container to the others, taking it back as soon as they had helped themselves, and started the process over again. They didn't seem in much of a hurry and they weren't eating very ravenously. The man calculated that the container must have been big enough to hold a good amount of food, which still wasn't much for three surely undernourished children.

A car appeared on the corner, driving slowly, as if looking for an address, and disappeared at the next corner. The four boys followed it with their eyes.

Up to that moment, none of them had said a single word. From the window, the man saw the biggest boy pass the food to his friend on the right, turn around, and say something the man couldn't hear. The other two also turned around. The three were still sitting on the curb, but they were now facing the boy at the gate behind them, less than ten feet away. The man couldn't tell if the boy replied or if he had in fact been the first to speak. After a few seconds, the three boys turned back around and started eating again, but only the two youngest partook. The oldest kept looking at the same thing the other boy was watching. There wasn't anything especially interesting there, just the white wall around the house across the street.

In a quick gesture, the oldest boy got up and pointed his finger at the boy by the gate. The man understood that he was telling the boy to get up. He got up. The two boys who were on the curb also got up and stood a ways off. The oldest boy was thin and drawn, much taller and older than the one he faced. The two stood without saying a word. The older boy's tense body contrasted with the casual attitude of the boy by the gate, who stood with his arms hanging by his sides.

Without warning, the older boy walked forward and unleashed a punch in the younger boy's face. From the window, the man could see the perplexed expression on the boy's face, even as his arms still hung in the same position. He looked to the side, as if seeking help from passersby, a lady across the street, an ice-cream man or dry cleaner; he looked at the windows of his house in search of his father and mother, but no sound emerged from his mouth, and there was nobody on the street. From a distance, he saw the man, but he was far off and hadn't moved from the window. The boy stood there with his arms hanging at his sides. When the older boy realized that there was no counterattack coming, nor even a defensive posture on the part of his adversary, he punched him again, and then a third time, each time in the face; the boy's nose was bleeding and his lip was cut. The older boy beat the younger, but the younger offered not the least bit of resistance. The man tried to cry from the window, but the sound came out weakly. He started to move his arms desperately and uselessly, paralyzed from meaningful action by his confusion. The older boy turned around, said something to the other two boys, and the three moved away unhurriedly in the direction they had come from, leaving their empty food container next to the curb.

The boy was still frozen, looking straight ahead, bleeding from the nose and mouth, his arms dangling from his body. After a while, he turned around, went back through the gate, and entered his house.

Espinosa could clearly make out the sounds coming from the street and was fully aware that he was lying in his own bed, but he still hadn't made up his mind to open his eyes. He tried to estimate the time: after six, for sure, so six-thirty was a good guess. He could have looked at the watch on his bedside table, which rested inches from his head, but that would mean accepting that he was technically awake. He kept his eyes closed. All he wanted at that time was, slowly, lazily, to enjoy the image of Irene coming up the two flights of stairs, arms full of bags, announcing what cheeses, wines, and bread she had brought; while he, at the top of the stairs, could look at her lightweight outfit hugging her thighs, her calves, and her breasts, insinuating more than showing. The imaginary scene wasn't borrowed from the night before or from any night in particular, recent or remote; it was a foretaste of the meeting they would have that night. Which was why he was reluctant to open his eyes and meet the stupid reality of his watch. It read six-twenty when Espinosa decided to get up.

He was turning on the coffeemaker when the telephone rang.

"Morning, Chief, sorry to wake you."

"You didn't. What happened?"

"A man was killed with a single shot at the end of the

Rua Mascarenhas de Moraes, that steep part off of the Rua Tonelero. We thought you'd like to see the body before it's removed."

"There's nothing to like about it, Detective."

"Sorry, just a manner of speaking."

"And why did you think I would like to see it? Is the victim someone I know?"

"No, sir, it's a homeless man, an old guy, with only one leg. . . . He was killed with a shot to his chest."

"A single shot?"

"Just one. Close range. In the heart. In the middle of a rainy night. He was stretched out at the end of the street . . . at that round end . . ."

"The cul-de-sac."

"Sorry?"

"It's called a cul-de-sac . . . it's French."

"Well, anyway, he had fallen beside that curb, and he was found by the doorman of the only building on that end of the street. I'm going to send a car to get you; it's raining and it's hard to get over there without a car."

"So how did he get there?"

"Exactly. . . . Nobody knows."

Even before the car went up the steep street, Espinosa recognized it. In his mind it wasn't the Rua Marechal Mascarenhas de Moraes but Otto's Street. That wasn't the street's original name, but when he was thirteen years old he and his friends always called it Otto's Street. They never saw a sign bearing that name, nor knew anyone on the street named Otto, nor was Otto some teenage idol of theirs. For whatever unknown reason, one day one of them decided to refer to it as Otto's Street, and the name stuck. Thirty years on, there he was, without the English bicycle that was the most incredible present his father ever gave him, recalling the intense emotion he felt before descending the street on that bicycle and feeling sadness at seeing the one-legged man, shot in the chest, fallen in the middle of the street. The geography was the same, but the stories were different.

The street was a steep, S-shaped road on the rocky flank of São João Hill, in Copacabana, entirely paved with cobblestones. Two sweeping curves along its four-hundred-meter length demanded careful attention from both drivers and pedestrians. The street began on the Rua Tonelero and ended in a little square that had once offered perfect views of most of Copacabana and the sea. Now the views were blocked by an apartment building that had been put up on the far side of the street, turning the cul-de-sac into a dark, charmless hole. One side of the cul-de-sac was bordered by a natural stone wall, almost entirely covered by vegetation. Alongside this wall, there was an old cement staircase that began at the entrance to the cul-de-sac and followed the curve of the hill until disappearing into the neighboring trees. The access to the staircase, a little gate hacked into the rock, was obstructed by a robust wooden door. The other side of the little square, which once faced the sea, was completely blocked off by a high masonry wall and the five stories of the building. There was also an iron gate, much larger than the first, that led to a plot of land that followed the slope of the hill down to the Rua Tonelero, two hundred meters down, and that belonged to a religious educational institution. The cul-de-sac was used almost exclusively by the residents of the street.

The body was lying at a point where the sidewalk hugged the stone wall. The plastic sack stretched across the body was not long enough to cover the wasted shin and the single foot, from the big toe of which hung a sandal worn out at the heel. Two crutches had been placed on top of the plastic, holding it down.

The nearest building was only a few meters away, shoe-horned into the space left by the neighboring constructions, luxurious mansions that had escaped the trend of tearing everything down to make room for apartment blocks. The garageman and the doorman employed there had already answered the questions from the policeman who had answered the call. The garageman, who had found the body, waited impatiently and curiously for the other cop, the one without a uniform who had arrived in a different car and seemed more important than the others, to call him over. But for the time being the policeman was more interested in the cobblestones, the curb, and in the little things he found on the ground and placed in a plastic bag. After that, he examined the dead man's pockets, moving on to explore beneath his shirt and inside his shorts. Finally, he took the crutches and examined them with the same care he had expended on the clothes. If he was looking for something in particular, he didn't find it. The man had already been engaged in his search for more than an hour when a car arrived, the same one that had brought him there, and deposited two men who were also in plain-clothes and carrying umbrellas. They greeted the other man immediately. Only then did they look in the direction of the garageman and head over to talk to him. The man who had been looking for things on the ground spoke.

"Good morning. I'm Chief Espinosa, from the Twelfth Precinct. This is Inspector Ramiro and Detective Welber. What is your name?"

"Severino."

"Are you the one who found the body?"

"Yes, sir."

"What time was it?"

"It was still dark. It must have been before five."

"And what were you doing outside, in the dark, while it was raining?"

"I'm the night doorman and also take care of the cars. I wash and drive them. When the garage is full I have to take one or two of the cars and park them outside, so that I can have the others ready in the order that the residents leave. It was when I took out the first car that the lights picked out the body lying on the ground. I immediately thought he was dead. If he had just been drunk, the rain would have woken him up."

"And then you went to make sure he was really dead?"

"I left the lights on and walked over. The rain had washed away the blood, but I could see the shot in the middle of his chest. I came back and called the police."

"You didn't touch the body?"

"No, sir."

"While you were washing the cars, you didn't hear a shot, or a car driving down the street?"

"It was raining hard, with thunder, and I didn't leave the garage until it was time to arrange the cars."

"Was anyone else in the garage with you?"

"No, sir."

"Did you know the dead man?"

"I'd seen him around, but I don't know who he is. I recognized him because of the leg . . ."

"Do you know what he was doing up here?"

"I think the people from the club might give him some food at the end of the day."

"What club?"

"The Horizon Club. It's right over there, behind that building, near the turnoff."

"You mean that every day he climbs up this street with only one leg? Even in the rain?"

They were talking beneath the door of the building's garage, and Severino repeatedly glanced inside the garage as he wrung the towel he used to dry the cars.

"Are you worried about something?" Espinosa asked.

"No, sir. It's just that one of the residents could come by and ask for their car."

"That's fine, Severino, thanks for your help. Detective Welber will take note of your name and phone number, in case we need to talk to you again. If you remember anything else, here's my card—you can call me at any time."

The rain had temporarily relented and the three went back over to the body. Espinosa made a broad gesture with his arms, indicating the cul-de-sac.

"I went over this entire area, every cobblestone, and I didn't find a single shell," he said.

"The murderer could have used a revolver, not a pistol."

"Or he made sure to pick up the shell. . . . Which doesn't sound like drug traffickers, since they don't care about those details; besides, with them it's rarely just a single shot. Soon the residents are going to start leaving for work. Make sure to ask them if they saw or heard anything, and come back later to talk to the ones who stay at home. Try the night owls and the insomniacs."

The police car that had responded to the doorman's call was still parked beside the curb, the lights on the roof blinking, in front of the car from the Twelfth Precinct. If any other car tried to turn around there, the driver would have a hard time getting down the narrow street, since the cul-de-sac was blocked with yellow police tape. Espinosa knew the body wouldn't be removed before noon, and that the forensic people wouldn't have much to do there—the rain that had been pouring down all night had washed out the crime scene.

"I'll see you back at the station. Keep the car. I want to go back on foot."

The twisting descent and the wet sidewalk forced Espinosa to pay attention so as not to slip while he was observing the neighboring houses. The club was at the corner of the hill, just off the street and protected by a wall with an entrance for cars and pedestrians. The club hadn't existed in the days of his adventures on his bicycle. In fact, few houses remained from that time—most of them had been replaced by little apartment buildings that occupied almost the entire length of the hill. Espinosa kept going downhill, experimenting with hopping down the tightest, most dangerous curves on a single leg. He could imagine that even with crutches, it wouldn't have been easy at all for the homeless man to climb up and go down the street. He kept walking, imagining what would lead a person with difficulty in walking to go beg in such a tough-to-reach spot, with little visibility, on a rainy night. As he walked the three more blocks to the Twelfth Precinct, he came up with a few answers to the question. None was satisfactory.

Neither the question nor the possible replies were anything like a real investigation, but they did increase the number of conjectures that told him that in his own head something was about to begin. He still couldn't call it an investigation: it was more like an intellectual stew combining very acute observations, subtle rationalizations, and delirious ideas. He considered it to be something like prethought, and—to his own relief and that of his colleagues—it was a passing phase . . . though it could occasionally bear useful fruit.

He would try not to think about it until Welber and Ramiro got back, around lunchtime. Since he didn't like to talk about cases he was working on while he ate, they probably wouldn't discuss the subject until the afternoon, which didn't mean that other ideas wouldn't occur to him in the meantime.

Camila and Aldo had different ways of waking up in the morning. While she took her time, languidly, step by step, stretching like a cat, he got up brusquely, tensely, going directly from sleep to a state of absolute alertness. And on that Friday morning he got up first. It was six-thirty. He turned off the alarm, which was set for seven, got up without making noise, and went into the bathroom. When he returned to the bedroom, having already showered and shaved, Camila was in the middle of her waking ritual, which would last another half hour. They had been married for more than ten years and he had never ceased to be fascinated by the way his wife rose from sleep. No other, up till then, was her match in beauty and sensuality, though these traits were not immediately obvious. They slowly became apparent to the spectator, until he was hopelessly captured by the fascination of Camila. He then went to wake the children, whose morning style was completely different from their parents'. Neither languor nor tension but resistance: they struggled for the right to one more minute in bed despite their father's kisses and words. Cíntia was like her mother in every way: pretty, charming, and as seductive as her nine years allowed her to be; Fernando, a year younger, was as intelligent as his sister but quieter. They studied full-time in a bilingual school. During the week they all ate breakfast together. When the school bus came to pick them up, it was still raining.

"Well?" said Camila as she scanned the newspaper.

"Well what?"

"Last night, during dinner, you were chatting up a storm . . . and on the way home you didn't say a single word and went to sleep without so much as a good night."

"Sorry. It's just that once the dinner was over I took off my costume. I was discouraged, tired of having to pretend that those spoiled kids were intelligent and interesting when in fact they're just talking dolls."

"But those talking dolls have the money to pay the best interior decorator in Rio de Janeiro."

"I did what they asked. The only thing I did was get rid of the obvious absurdities and add a few of my own ideas."

"So there you have it. That's the magic of your profession: getting them to think that those were their ideas."

"Then they could cut out the dinner parties to show off their new house."

"But, honey, they also want to show off the new designer. We agreed, it's good for their ego and it's good for yours as well . . . and for your wallet."

"They didn't even see the money! The money went straight from her father's account to mine."

"Even better: from the source. But you still haven't told me why you came home depressed. Was it something someone said?"

"I don't know what it was, but it's over now. Are you going to go to work now?"

"No, today I only have patients in the afternoon. This morning I'm going to take care of my body and my hair."

"We can go out for dinner, just the two of us, if you can find someone to stay with the kids."

Aldo and Camila lived in one of the most sought-after blocks in Ipanema, halfway between the beach and the lagoon and two blocks from the Jardim de Alá. Camila walked to her office and to everything she most required for her personal well-being. She didn't need to have her girlfriends around to go shopping, work out, or check out the latest publications in the neighborhood bookstore. She only liked groups on birthdays and for small dinner parties; besides that, she liked to be alone or with her husband. The gym not only kept her body in shape but also cleared her head of the unpleasant aspects of daily life.

She liked to go after eight in the morning, when the first wave of visitors, who had to be at work by nine, were already gone and the group of people who got up later had yet to arrive. And the rainy morning didn't seem to beckon people to leave home to go to the gym, or at least that's what she gathered when she found that even the most popular machines were free. An hour of working out was exactly what she needed. When she left the gym, already showered, the rain had stopped and the shops were opening. She liked to wander through the shopping centers, entering stores, lingering in the bookstore, or trying on clothes, usually returning home empty-handed. By eleven she was at the hairdresser's and at twelve-thirty she ate a salad on the terrace of a neighborhood restaurant. At two o'clock she saw the day's first patient.

Aldo, as soon as he started booking clients as an interior architect (he didn't like being called a decorator), rented an apartment and set up his office on the Avenida Atlântica, facing the sea, in an old building that made a very favorable impression on his clients. He worked with Mercedes, a young architect who had recently graduated, and two architecture students around twenty years old, Rafaela and Henrique, who served as interns. When he was working on more than one project or developing others, he brought in extra help. He wasn't interested in a big office with a permanent team of specialists; he preferred to concentrate on a small group under his direction. He wanted people to come for Aldo Bruno, architect, rather than Bruno Interior Architecture Inc. or something along those lines. Moreover, the building was residential, and he couldn't hang out a sign with the name of the firm. But nothing prevented him from affixing to the door a little bronze plaque the size of a business card, with his name engraved in elegant black letters. As far as the building knew, it wasn't an architecture firm but a private studio.

His professional success had begun with a dinner Camila had given in her parents' house to introduce her husband to a group of their friends she had selected, all of whom were very rich and whose children were around her age. The dinner was followed by brief encounters with their children, all of whom were interested in redecorating. The next time Camila invited them to their own home and left her parents out of it. The effort wouldn't have succeeded without his talent, of course.

Around twelve-thirty, just as Camila was having lunch in Ipanema, Aldo left for lunch in the Japanese restaurant next to his building.

The weather improved over the course of the morning. Around noon there was already more blue sky than clouds. When Ramiro and Welber came back to meet the boss and head out to lunch, the strong sun was already drying the sidewalks. Ramiro told the story.

"Chief, nobody in the building or in the houses nearby heard or saw anything, but in one of the houses near the building, the third from the place where the body was found, there was a party or a dinner that wrapped up around two in the morning. We talked with the servants, since the owners were asleep. They had moved in that week, after months of work. Last night they gave a dinner to show the house to their friends and to honor the architect who did the house, a man named Aldo Bruno. There were fourteen people, besides the owners of the house."

"Of course the guests came by car," said Espinosa. "Seven or eight cars, five of which must have been parked on either side of the street and maybe two up in the cul-de-sac. This morning I noticed that lots of residents park on the street, which leaves few places for visitors, and all of them have to turn around at the end of the street. If nobody saw anything, that means the crime occurred after the last guests had departed. Go back to the house after lunch and get the names and phone numbers of everybody who was at the dinner, and find out who were the last to leave."

They walked down the Rua Hilário de Gouveia and turned left onto the Avenida Copacabana, heading toward the trattoria on the Rua Fernando Mendes where Espinosa ate whenever he could escape the usual routine of sandwiches and milkshakes. Ramiro and Welber couldn't eat in a restaurant every day, even when it was a cheap place like the trattoria. That was especially true for Welber, a lower-ranking detective who was carefully saving money for a down payment on an apartment in the Zona Sul of Rio where he and his girlfriend, Selma, could move after they got married. Inspector Ramiro, head of the detectives, earned a bit more money, but he had a wife and kids. For the two cops, who lived in the Zona Norte and had a long commute to the Twelfth Precinct in Copacabana, eating out every day in a restaurant wasn't sensible, especially since they were the kind of cops who didn't accept certain types of favors from businessmen. But that was exactly the reason that they were perhaps the only ones Espinosa trusted unreservedly.

Since they didn't talk about work during lunch, the conversation eventually led Espinosa to reminisce about his childhood adventures on the street where the crime took place.

"It was just after we'd moved from Saúde, downtown, to the Peixoto District. Funny . . . neither of the neighborhoods of my childhood were actually neighborhoods, but something like quasi-neighborhoods or little areas inside a real neighborhood. Anyway, my father bought an apartment in the Peixoto District, where we moved when I was nine. When I turned ten, I got a Raleigh bicycle, English made, which was the best present I ever got in my entire life. With it, I started to explore the area. At first, the Peixoto District itself, a world as protected as a medieval city, and unthreatening; as time went by, the world extended to include all of Copacabana. That's when my friends and I discovered Otto's Street. That's what we called it. We decided to explore the place: we wanted to know where it ended up and then ride down it, controlling the speed of our bikes with the brakes and our nerves. We could only ride up to the first curve; after that, we had to push the bikes up. By the second or third try, we went up to the end of the street, which at the time had no buildings around it—only a low stone wall where we could sit to admire the marvelous view of Copacabana with the sea behind it. After that, it became our secret place, which, besides the view, offered the prize of the dizzying descent down to the Rua Tonelero."

"And they let you ride your bike around Copacabana when you were ten?"

"Well, as you know, my parents died in a car crash a few months after my birthday. I was raised by my grandmother, the only relative I had left. She didn't let me leave the

Peixoto District. But when I was thirteen she let me go to the nearby streets—that's when we discovered Otto's Street."

"So that's why . . ."

"That's why I'm interested in the victim."

Since Espinosa didn't say anything else, the other two changed the subject and began discussing another recurring theme in their lunches: the advantages and disadvantages of living in Copacabana. Ramiro and Welber lived on the border of Grajaú and Méier, in the northern part of the city, "miles away from everything interesting in Rio," as Welber put it.

"Like what, for example?" Ramiro wanted to know.

"Jesus, Ramiro, the beaches, the bars, the restaurants, the shops, Copacabana, Ipanema, Leblon, the nightlife . . . and the day life, too, of course, with those hot women in bikinis right in front of your face. . . . What do you want? The romance of the far reaches? This is the greatest! And it's free! If you've got any doubts, walk out of the restaurant, go a hundred feet to the corner of the Avenida Atlântica, and look around. That's all. Look around. Then try the same thing in Grajaú or Méier."

Back at the station, the conversation returned to business. There were two questions Espinosa thought demanded a response. The first: What would have led a man over fifty years old, poor, fragile, missing a leg, walking with the aid of crutches, to climb up that steep street on a rainy night?

And the second: Who would have needed to go up that same street, on foot or by car, to kill, with such efficiency and precision, that poor guy?

"I'd like you to return to the Horizon Club. Talk with the cleaning people and the kitchen staff. Someone's got to know who the dead man was. Then go back to the house that was just refurbished, talk to the owners, and get a list of everyone who was there last night. And then, at the end of the afternoon, see if you can get any news from the Forensic Institute. Even if it's off the record."

The visit to the club proved fruitful. The employees knew the victim and were sad about his death. They spoke of the subject openly.

"We don't know hardly anything about him. Just that he was homeless and that he had trouble finding work because of his leg."

"Do you know his name?"

"Ever since he showed up here, we've called him Skinny. I don't know his real name."

"And how did he end up here?"

"One of the employees who knew him said that when there were parties there was always a lot of food that got tossed out. And that if he showed up late at night, he could get him some. After that, he showed up whenever there was a party."

"What's the name of this fellow? Can we talk to him?"

"His name is Joca. He doesn't work here anymore."

"How did the homeless guy manage to climb up here with crutches?"

"Joca knew him from the Pavãozinho slum. He said that Skinny climbed up and down the hill on his crutches."

"How often did he come here, and how did he get in?"

"He only came every once in a while, every two weeks or so, and he didn't come into the club. He waited for us to take the trash out to the gate and then he asked for something to eat. We filled up a plate for him and then he took it to eat somewhere else."

"He never mentioned if he had any family or anyone he hung around with?"

"He didn't talk much. All we know about him was from when Joca still worked here."

"Did he have any enemies?"

"What do you mean?"

"Anyone who wanted to get back at him for any reason . . ."

"Who knows? I don't think so. He was just a poor guy who didn't threaten anybody."

"If you remember anything else, call me," Ramiro said. "The number's on this card."

From the club Welber and Ramiro proceeded to the house that had hosted the dinner party, almost directly opposite the entrance to the club. There, the two policemen found their task more difficult. After having to badger the same servants they had spoken to that morning, they managed to get the lady of the house to appear at the gate. The woman who greeted them looked more like a teenager scared by the appearance of the police than the owner of a mansion.

"My husband just left" was the first thing she said, as soon as she saw the cops.

"Good morning, ma'am, I'm Inspector Ramiro and this is Detective Welber, from the Twelfth Precinct, and we need your help. . . . Afterward we'll speak to your husband."

"The servants said there was a crime here on the street."

"That's true."

"They killed a poor . . ."

"That's right, they killed a homeless man . . ."

"Ah."

"With a shot to the chest."

"And what does that have to do with us?"

"You and your husband can help us determine the approximate time the crime was committed."

"How?"

"You gave a dinner last night for fourteen people."

"Seven couples."

"That's what we figured. And every couple must have come in their own car . . ."

"That's right. Nobody came in a taxi and nobody came together."

"Great. So there were seven cars parked here in the street. I suppose that the guests all left at different times?"

"Right. But I still don't know what this has to do with the crime."

"Since the street is so narrow," Ramiro said, "the cars have to turn around at the end of the block, fifty meters from your house."

"That's true."

"Well, the body was found up there at the end of the street. We want to know if any of the guests, when they were turning around, saw the man. Dead or alive. If he was alive, it would be easy to recognize him because he only had one leg and used crutches. If he was dead, same thing: he had fallen onto the sidewalk, next to the stone wall."

"And what do you want from me?"

"The guest list, and their telephone numbers."

"But I can't do that!"

"Why, ma'am?"

"Because they're my guests. I can't give out their names to the police for some homeless man."

"A homeless man who was murdered, ma'am."

"I have to speak to my father or my husband."

"Whatever you want, ma'am."

The woman consulted her father and her husband over the phone; they consulted their attorneys, who made a series of recommendations to the couple and demands to the policemen, who only at the end of the afternoon got the list of the guests who had come to the dinner driving their own cars. Six men and a woman. One of the men didn't know how to drive. Of the seven drivers, three, including the woman, had made the turn at the end of the street when they'd arrived, so that they would be facing the exit when they left. The four others drove into the cul-de-sac as they were departing. None saw the homeless man. Neither alive nor dead.

At the end of the afternoon, Freire, a researcher at the Carlos Éboli Institute of Criminology, called Espinosa. The two had entered the police force together—Espinosa as a detective and Freire as a researcher. Over the course of the two decades since then, they had become friends—a friendship that people who knew them found improbable, since Espinosa was a master of verbal elegance and Freire, for his part, eliminated all adjectives, adverbs, prepositions, pronouns, and such, employing in his speech only nouns and verbs. Currently, moreover, he was tending to eliminate verbs as well. So when Espinosa picked up the phone, all he heard was:

"Thirty-eight."

2

In summertime, it was common for patients who lived in the neighborhood to show up in shorts, T-shirts, and sandals, stretching out on the analytic couch as if relaxing on a neighbor's sofa for a chat with a friend. Maria was one such patient. She had started her analysis three months before, and despite the appearance of comfort that her casual attire and informal manners gave her, she was still stuck in the narrative of her life. Thirty-something, attractive, with a story of sexual disinterest for her husband and for men in general. She had two daughters, who were now twelve and nine; she lived comfortably and worked for herself, painting textiles and creating exclusive patterns for Ipanema boutiques. She spoke little and softly, but her face and body were expressive. She took off her sandals to stretch out on the couch and often managed to be more eloquent with her feet than with her hands. Camila sat in a chair slightly behind the couch, allowing her a full view of the patient's body, while the patient, reclining, could see only a bit of the analyst's leg and feet . . . unless she sat up or lay flat. But she hadn't gotten there yet.

Maria was the first patient that afternoon. She always got there on time, came in without saying anything, took off her sandals and lay down. She'd remain silent for a few minutes, then try out a few words, a sentence or two, and after that pick up the more or less linear narrative she had interrupted in the last session. At the most intense moments, her breathing changed and the points of her breasts pushed up the T-shirt she was wearing without a bra, while her feet executed a looping dance, coming apart and then lovingly rubbing up against each other. Camila never saw her body still. Every part of Maria was expressive—it could be a muscle on her leg that flexed, or the long fingers that played with a bit of her black hair—though in that context speech was the most important thing.

Twenty minutes into the session, Camila placed her hand close to Maria's hair, almost touching it. She wanted to see if there was any reaction on the part of the patient, though the patient could not see her hand. Then she touched a bit of the hair that was resting on the back of the couch. There was no reaction . . . and Camila didn't do anything else. Until the last patient left, at seven in the evening, she didn't think anything more about Maria.

The kids were already used to Ana, the babysitter, a plump, jolly college student who knew Cíntia and Fernando well and had a special knack for keeping them under control—and lived three blocks away, which made it easier to call on her at the last minute.

Aldo and Camila chose a restaurant they and their friends rarely visited. On the way, they almost didn't speak.

Aldo made a couple of unimportant comments, and Camila didn't ask any questions or try to keep the conversation going. After they were seated, she asked up front:

"Honey, what's going on?"

Aldo hesitated, and Camila went on.

"Because obviously something is worrying you . . . and it has to do with the dinner last night."

"That's true. I just don't know what it is."

"What do you mean?"

"There's something that's really bothering me, but I can't say what it is. I thought it had to do with the people at the dinner last night, the vapid conversation, the stupid interests of those people. But then I realized that wasn't it. I've been dealing with people like that for a long time. I know what they're like and how they think. They're not empty people. To the contrary. It's almost as if they had no emptiness at all inside them. Their desires have hardly arrived and they are already satisfied. That used to bother me, but it doesn't anymore. So then I thought it was the call from the police."

"The police called you?"

"They did. They found the body of a beggar, shot to death at the end of the Rua Mascarenhas de Moraes, where I parked the car last night. The cops wanted to know if I had seen the beggar or his body. From what I could make out, they spoke to all the guests at the party to see if they could determine the hour of the crime. But apparently nobody saw anything."

"Especially in that weather. You were soaking wet."

"But that wasn't it either . . . I already felt bad long before that call."

"Anything to do with the people at the dinner?"

"I didn't know any of them."

"So could it have something to do with me?"

"Don't even think that. You're the best thing that ever happened to me." He stretched out his hand and rubbed his wife's arm.

"Then let's order and try to relax."

The food was delicious, the wine adequate, and they didn't return to the subject. But Aldo couldn't relax. Something was still tormenting him.

After the call from the Criminological Institute confirmed that the bullet removed from the beggar's body was from a thirty-eight revolver, Espinosa turned off his computer, removed his weapon and his wallet from the drawer, put on his coat, went downstairs, and passed through the arch-shaped door of the Twelfth Precinct without looking at anyone, fearing a last-minute communication that would keep him at the station. Nobody called him, there was no car bearing a suspected murderer parked in front of the station, and his cell phone didn't ring, asking him to come to an emergency meeting at the Department of Security. Nothing. He was entirely free for the already-confirmed encounter he would have with Irene that very night. He was in Rio, Irene was in Rio, which wasn't always the case, and both were free. It didn't often happen that way:

sometimes weeks went by without their seeing each other, speaking only over the phone. But that night, it seemed, nothing was going to get in their way.

More than ten years separated Espinosa and Irene: he was forty-three, and she had just barely hit thirty; and he thought that a decade was enough to produce a discontinuity, if not a rupture, in the ways lovers spoke to each other. Not that the decades were rigid bands allowing no kind of communication between them, but he suspected that there was a kind of barrier that would not exist with someone one's own age. The simple fact of having that thought—on his way home, and as he showered—was an irrefutable sign that he was getting older. The distance between their ages didn't remain arithmetically constant but grew with each passing year. At first, it was a twelve-year gap, and now it felt more like fifteen or even twenty years. He let the water run down his body as he looked at himself. He hadn't gotten fat, his abdomen was still well defined, the little tire that was growing around his waist was negligible, he wasn't bald and he hadn't gone gray—besides the occasional hair on his temples—and his muscles and joints still worked. The problem was that when he thought about Irene, that little inventory felt like an autopsy. Irene was life at its peak. In his most self-deprecating moments he compared them to a roller coaster: Irene at the top of the curve and he at the end of the first descent, with no way back, on his way to the ground . . . or underground, he thought. But he didn't say any of this to her. He was her knight in shining armor. He just didn't know for how long.

Though it was summer, the unending rain of the last few days had brought the temperature down to below average. Bad weather for tourists, but great for someone who wanted to spend time at home with a lover.

Irene's arrival was auspicious. She hugged and kissed Espinosa even before putting down the bags she had loaded with enough wine, bread, and cheese to transform the night into a bacchanalia.

From the beginning of their relationship, the two had agreed that they would always meet in his apartment. Irene was a graphic designer who had spent time at MoMA in New York at an age when most of her colleagues in the field were still interns trapped in Rio and São Paulo. She had her own apartment in Ipanema—not a big one but nicely decorated, though a bit formal for Espinosa's taste. That's why they'd elected his apartment for their rendezvous. Informal, simple, without notable works of art, but charming and pleasant.

Irene described the merits of every item she removed from the bags—wines, cheeses, cold cuts, and breads of various descriptions—and showed them to Espinosa as if presenting them at an auction. He indicated his approval of each one and kissed Irene on a different part of her body; and, as he always did when she was performing that pantomime, he interrupted the show when the kisses reached places that forced her to wrap up the performance.

Back in the living room, a towel around his waist, he

finished unloading the bags. He was placing two bottles of wine in the refrigerator and unwrapping the cheeses and cold cuts when she came out of the bedroom wearing nothing but her panties. She stood beside him to help.

Espinosa's building was on the square at the heart of the Peixoto District. Almost all the buildings in the area had no more than four stories and the same architectural style. Luckily for Espinosa, his apartment had French windows with Venetian blinds and glass that went from floor to ceiling. The windows opened out onto a little balcony less than three feet wide and with wrought-iron railings. On that night, because of the rain that had started to fall again, he only closed the blinds, to let a little air in and to keep the neighbors from seeing what was going on inside the apartment. Thanks to that precaution, Irene could walk around almost entirely nude, which she did with a brazenness that perturbed Espinosa.

"Irene . . . you're creating an absurd conflict of interests . . ."

"Just because I'm not wearing a bra?"

"My dear, it's entirely impossible for me to pay attention to anything else with you all but naked by my side."

"Then I'll stand behind you . . . so you can keep doing whatever it was you were busy with."

"I just can't."

"But we've been naked for more than an hour."

"True, but then we were screwing. I can't eat bread or cheese with you naked on my lap."

"I'm not on your lap."

"You might as well be."

Espinosa sought in vain any news about the homeless man's death in the police pages of the Saturday morning papers. Nothing about that death was news: an old crippled beggar killed on a dead-end street beside a hill in Copacabana on a stormy night. . . . The man, who was almost elderly, who looked sick, was missing a leg, unarmed, and a threat to nobody, besides having no apparent connection to drug traffickers. . . . He was killed with a single shot to the middle of his chest, and that intrigued Espinosa. More than intrigued: the chief was shocked, saddened, and provoked by it.

"What happened, babe, you didn't have fun last night?"

"Of course I did . . ."

"So why are you knitting your brows? You still haven't had your coffee."

"I was waiting for you to get up."

"And in the meantime you read something in the paper that bothered you."

"What do you want for breakfast? We still have the Italian bread from last night, all sorts of cheeses, delicious cold cuts, eggs in the fridge. And there's also regular bread. My toaster will only toast one side of the bread at a time, so you have to do it in two steps . . . but it's a thrill when they finally bounce up perfectly toasted."

"I'm going to have black coffee and try to experience the thrilling adventure of toast in the morning."

"It's unforgettable."

"Now tell me why you were looking so worried after everything we did last night."

While he was filling the coffeemaker, Espinosa briefly told her about the homeless man.

"And what's worrying you about it?"

"The gratuitousness of the murder. The excess."

"Did you know him?"

"I have a vague notion that I've seen him before. Maybe because of the crutches. But there's also something else. . . . The tense, long face . . . still with both legs. It's also that the cul-de-sac is one of the secret places of my childhood."

"Maybe that's why it affected you so much."

"Maybe."

When Aldo left his bedroom the next morning, Cíntia and Fernando were already awake and ready to go to the club, just like they did every Saturday.

"Dad, are you going to take us to the club?"

"Let's wait for your mother to get up."

"She can come later. We'll leave Fernando here to come with her and the two of us can go now."

"Forget it. You and your brother are going together, and Mom is coming with us."

"But nobody stays together. Fernando goes off to play

with his bratty little friends, and you and Mom stay with the adults . . ."

". . . and you hang out with your friends."

"But Mom is still asleep! It'll take her forever, and it's not raining today, so everyone's already there. It's almost ten and we're still not even ready . . ."

"If you want to go out so badly, call your brother and we'll go down to the kiosk and get a paper."

"The papers are already here, they're all on the table."

"I want to buy other ones."

"More of the same?"

"No, sweetie, different ones."

"Okay."

"So go get your brother."

The three walked the block to a kiosk on the Rua Visconde de Pirajá. Besides the papers Aldo bought, the kids got magazines and collectible envelopes with comic-strip characters, gum, and a sticker for each one. When they got home, Camila was drinking her coffee.

"Mom, look at my sticker."

"And my comic-strip characters, Mom."

"And you, what kind of paper is that? Didn't our papers come?"

"They did. I wanted to check out the other ones."

"What other ones?"

"The more . . . popular ones."

"What are you looking for?"

The kids had gone off to read their magazines and comics.

"What's going on, Aldo? Are you still thinking about what happened a couple of nights ago?"

"I went to get the papers with crime news. I wanted to know what happened at the end of that street. But on the way I looked and there's nothing. Maybe I didn't look carefully enough. I'm going to look again."

"For what?"

"I'm not sure. To figure out what happened. After all, the cops called the office asking if I had seen anything. I don't know what 'anything' they're talking about. They mentioned a beggar on crutches. Then they mentioned a dead man . . ."

"But, Aldo, what does this have to do with you? You didn't see anything, and that's the end of it."

"It's not as simple as that."

"Why not? Did you see anything? No! Finished. Over. It's not your problem. It's the police's problem. We're going to take the kids to the club, work out for a few minutes, have a sauna and a shower. And then we'll try to find a quiet place where we can talk about what's bothering you. How does that sound?"

Monday morning, and the first news Espinosa got was an e-mail from the Forensic Institute reporting on the autopsy of the homeless man known as Skinny. Summing up: the projectile hit his heart, instant death; no sign in his body of drugs, alcohol, or food. The examiner used other terms, but that was how Espinosa translated it.

"He didn't even get to eat," he mumbled to himself.

He was all alone in his office. He printed out the message and sat staring at the paper, reading and rereading the text, until Welber and Ramiro arrived.

"Morning, Chief," they both said at the same time.

Espinosa showed them the e-mail and repeated the comment he had just made to himself.

"No drugs or alcohol," Ramiro noted. "He didn't have anything to do with the drug dealers, according to the guy who worked at the club. Everything indicates that he really was a down-on-his-luck homeless guy that nobody would have a motive to kill. If we add that the weapon was a thirty-eight, which is almost as common as a kitchen knife, we don't have much to go on."

"Thirty-eight," Espinosa repeated. "That's why we didn't find the cartridge, and that's why we'll probably never find the weapon. And if we don't use our heads, we'll probably never find the murderer. Especially because we're the only ones who care: no paper ran a story about it and nobody claimed the body. When he's buried in the paupers' cemetery, we'll have a crime without a body, without a weapon, without a witness, without a clue, and without a motive. In other words, an investigation generally given zero priority."

"We talked to dozens of neighbors and servants. Nobody saw anything. We spoke with everyone at the dinner party who parked in the street. Only two of them parked in the cul-de-sac. Neither of them saw a thing."

"Well, they'll be our starting point," said Espinosa.

"Let's go back and talk to them again. Sometimes people don't say anything because they don't want to get involved in a police investigation. Let's ask them once again, making sure not to interrupt their daily routines."

"Chief, as soon as we ask them, they'll already be bothered."

"So we apologize and thank them for their help. Which ones were parked up there?"

"The architect who redid the house, Aldo Bruno, and a friend of the house's owner, Rogério Antunes."

"Which one left first?"

"Aldo Bruno left an hour before Rogério Antunes. The architect left just after dinner, but the last guests didn't leave until around one-thirty in the morning."

"What we need is the testimony of the two who were parked up at the end of the street, especially the last person to leave. Ask about the position of the cars, if they had to turn around, if their lights lit up the whole end of the street, if it was raining very hard when they got into the car, if they were using umbrellas. Ask if they use glasses or contact lenses and, most importantly, if they went to get their cars alone."

"We've already asked everyone if they saw anyone on crutches anywhere on the street, either coming up or going down. They all said it was raining and that the street was deserted. Only two of them met another car coming up: one was a taxi and another was a private car. They didn't see where the taxi stopped or where the other car entered.

As for the architect and Rogério Antunes, when we spoke to them on the phone they both said that there was nobody, alive or dead, with or without crutches."

"I'd like you to speak with them personally, not on the phone. I'd also like for both of you to be there for the interviews. Try to find that ex-employee of the Horizon Club, the one who told Skinny about the place."

Welber knew that the order to conduct the interviews together was meant to help him learn from Ramiro about interviewing and interrogating: the inspector was a master. Welber also knew that this talent was more than something you could get out of a training manual; it was a special talent, to get the interviewee to spill the beans. He'd already seen Ramiro in action and he had also been present at countless interviews conducted by Espinosa himself. They were never arrogant, they never suggested any physical threat, they spoke softly and in a friendly tone, and they were tireless. After a while, people started telling them things they wouldn't confess even to a close friend. Of course, that wasn't the usual way things went in a police station.

Ramiro had been in the force longer than Espinosa and was already counting down the days till retirement. Espinosa considered him a first-rate cop: a meticulous investigator and a skilled interrogator, but one who had never wanted to go to law school, which meant he'd never become the boss. Ramiro liked being an inspector. He was the leader of all the detectives in the precinct. He and Welber shared Espinosa's trust: the boss knew they were incorruptible. While Ramiro was older than the chief, Welber was twenty years younger. A detective third-class, he had once saved Espinosa's life and almost lost his own when he placed himself between the chief and a gunman in a hotel hallway. He got off with only a perforated spleen. Ever since then, they had worked together.

3

On Mondays and Thursdays, Camila saw a patient during lunchtime, a dentist who couldn't or didn't want to give up one of his own patients and had to come in at noon— Camila's usual lunch hour. His name was Faustino. Camila estimated him to be about as old as Aldo. He was a little stronger, but he wasn't as good-looking, principally because of a physical characteristic that bothered him and that had become a constant theme in their sessions: he had a very small forehead, his dense black hair almost touching his eyebrows, which, according to the dentist himself, made him look unintelligent. Faustino was monothematic and had at first described in great detail every one of his dental interventions, from a simple cavity to a prolonged, complex root canal. Now, ever since the issue of the small forehead had appeared, it came up in every session like a recurring, untreatable toothache. It not only offended his aesthetic sensibilities, it also reduced his chances with women, which left him annoyed and aggressive. From the stories of her patient's amorous conquests, Camila, ungraciously, had started to suspect that his forehead wasn't the only small thing about him.

After the appointment, she checked her messages. The only one was from Aldo. She called him immediately, and he picked up himself.

"Camila, those cops called again."

"And what did they want from you?"

"Apparently they just want to ask me and the other guy who was parked up there a few questions."

"You didn't answer them already?"

"I did, but they want to speak in person. They wanted to speak to you too, so I said that I got the car by myself."

"Which is true."

"So they said they would talk just to me. They're coming at two."

"They must just want for you to confirm what you said before. It'll give you time to have lunch."

"I'm not hungry."

"Why are you nervous?"

"I don't like the police."

"Neither do I, but we don't have anything to do with the death of that poor man. It must be routine. I'll call you back to find out how it went. Try to eat at least a sandwich."

She, too, went out to have something to eat. Nothing heavy or complicated, but she didn't want to go into her afternoon sessions on nothing more than breakfast. Camila had felt her husband's nervousness on the phone. She'd known Aldo for more than ten years, she knew he had nothing to fear from a meeting with the police, that he was an honest man who never got involved in anything illicit. She didn't understand why he was so nervous, though she thought it had something to do with the dinner party. Maybe someone had said something unpleasant. . . . Though he only knew the owners of the house. . . . Except that

46

people always manage to say rude things, even if they don't know one another, or precisely for that reason . . .

She found an empty table on the sidewalk in front of one of the recently opened restaurants in the neighborhood, asked for a house salad and a juice, and thought about her husband and the way he felt threatened by anything that exceeded the boundaries of his daily life. "Unknown" and "threatening" were practically synonymous for him. He didn't feel threatened by new events that appeared in the world of his family or job, but he could get extremely shaky when faced with anything unexpected. Professionally, he combined boldness with conformity, which earned him a good reputation among a clientele whose aesthetic sense was not overdeveloped. He never did anything in bad taste, but, out of fear of inciting displeasure, he had never dared to be the best in his field. And that was what touched her especially, that feeling that her husband was always playing it safe. It wasn't just in his professional life. It was something bigger than that, something undetermined. Even behind the happiness he showed when he was with his family or friends, there was always a hint of fear.

Her thoughts were interrupted by two men staring at her from a nearby table. They were looking and talking between themselves in a ridiculous pantomime of conquest. Middle-aged, probably the owners of some neighborhood shop, not physically unattractive but entirely bereft of charm. Typical machos whose main occupation, if not their exclusive occupation, was to conquer the females who appeared in their territory. Camila reflected that this was one of the biggest mistakes men made, and the few men who didn't were the truly interesting ones. Good-looking or not. And these two were definitely not very interesting. She paid the bill and went to meet her first patient of the afternoon.

Ramiro and Welber arrived at the building on the Avenida Atlântica a few minutes before two and had the doorman announce them. It was a residential building from the fifties with art deco details in the entryway hall. On the door of the apartment that housed Aldo's office-studio, the only clues were the number of the apartment and a plaque with the name Aldo Bruno in black letters. The architect himself opened the door.

"Sir, thank you so much for seeing us. I'm Inspector Ramiro and this is my colleague Detective Welber, from the Twelfth Precinct."

"Please, come in. My two interns are at lunch, so we're alone."

The office was simple and decorated in very good taste. Two large rooms faced the sea. The interns worked in the first, while the second was Aldo Bruno's office, where he received clients. The furniture was both elegant and functional. In the first room there were three tables with shiny new computers, filing cabinets, and shelves; in Aldo's office there was a conference table with a glass top and eight chairs, a computer table, and the only drawing board in the office.

"We don't want to take much of your time; it's just a couple of questions."

"As I said on the phone, I don't think there's much I can add to what I've already told you."

"Then it will be even quicker. Can you tell me exactly how you left the house to get your car, after the dinner party?"

"Well. We were the first to leave. It was raining heavily, so I told my wife to wait in the hallway of the house while I went to get the car."

"Why were you the first to leave? Did something happen during the dinner?"

"No, nothing. It was a nice dinner, but the other guests already knew each other and were a lot younger than we are. We didn't think we would be missed too much. Besides, it was late, it was after midnight."

"When you went to get the car, were you wearing a hood or holding an umbrella?"

"No, neither. When I got in the car, I was soaking wet."

"Did you see anyone on your way to the car?"

"No, the street was deserted."

"Was the car parked in front of the stone wall or the building?"

"The wall."

"And then . . ."

"I got in the car, started the engine, turned around, and picked up my wife."

"You didn't turn on the lights?"

"I did. It was dark, and that part of the street is badly lit."

"When you turned on the lights, you didn't see anything that grabbed your attention?"

"No. I just saw the rain and the rock covered with moss and plants."

"And then?"

"Then I picked up my wife, who was waiting out of the rain, and we went home."

"On the way down the street, did you see anyone coming up, or stopped on the curb?"

"As far as I can remember, nobody was on the street. As I said, it was late and it was pouring down rain."

"When you turned around in the dead end did you have your brights on?"

"No, but then I turned them on."

"The end of the street isn't more than ten meters across, which means that if you turned around to go back down your lights would have scanned the whole area. You didn't see a body on the ground?"

"No."

"A body that might have looked like a passed-out drunk?"

"I would have remembered if I'd seen it."

"Another thing: Do you keep a weapon in your glove compartment?"

"No."

"And at home, do you have a weapon?"

"No."

"Have you ever?"

"I did. But not anymore."

"What did you do with it?"

"My kids were getting older and I thought it was better not to have a gun in the house. I turned it in to be destroyed during a disarmament campaign."

"How long ago was this?"

"Around two years ago."

"Was it a revolver or a pistol?"

"A revolver."

"Do you remember what caliber?"

"Thirty-two. I handed in the weapon and the box of bullets. Both intact. I never fired a shot."

"Thanks so much, sir, and sorry for taking up your time."

In the elevator, they didn't say a word. As if there was anyone around who might hear the big secret Ramiro was about to reveal. But there wasn't one. On the street, without anyone around to overhear them, Welber asked:

"So, what did you think?"

"I didn't think anything, I just didn't like the last answer. He didn't need to say that he had turned in the gun and the bullets intact. 'I never fired a shot.' What does that mean, he never fired a shot? He bought a gun and a box of bullets and never tried firing even one little shot? Not even to hear what it sounded like? Besides, I asked if he had a gun, not whether he had fired at anyone or anything. 'I never fired a shot' didn't sound right. But nobody's going to end up in jail because they told a little white lie."

"There was one other thing that I noticed," said Welber.

"Fire away, buddy. What's on your mind?"

"The fact that he didn't ask a single question. I think it's pretty strange that a guy who meets two cops who are investigating a murder and doesn't ask a single question. Not even out of curiosity or politeness, like 'Can I get you a glass of water?' I thought he was pretty defensive, and that means there's something to protect."

"Very good, buddy, good observation."

"And now?"

"Now let's chat with Mr. Rogério Antunes, the other guy who was parked there at the end of the street."

Rogério Antunes was quite different from Aldo Bruno. He greeted the two men on the terrace of the Yacht Club, where he had just had lunch. Chatty, with a nice tan that he'd been working on for a long time, wearing shorts, a T-shirt, and moccasins, he asked countless questions about the crime and wanted to know everything about what the two policemen were up to. As for the scene of the crime, he had almost nothing to say.

"I had parked facing downhill, so when I went to get the car all I had to do was get in, turn on the engine and the lights, and go down. There wasn't another car around and I didn't see anyone. I didn't even bother to look, I just got in the car and left. I can also tell you exactly what time it was: one-thirty in the morning."

Ramiro and Welber left the club by the longest route, walking along the whole length of the anchorage, looking at the sailboats and the launches, admiring the beauty of the landscape of the Bay of Botafogo, with the Sugar Loaf a stone's throw away.

"Very nice guy. Sensational setting, perfectly receptive,

but the guy couldn't even tell if there was a cadaver lying in the street a few feet away."

"He's used to the sun and the sea, and his eyes can't adjust to the darkness of rainy nights," said Welber.

"Damn, Welber, stop enjoying yourself so much—we still haven't gotten any useful information. The only thing the guy is sure about is the time. So what? If he didn't see anything, knowing what time it was doesn't help us at all. Including the people who live in the building, the other houses, their employees and maids, there were at least a hundred people. None of them saw a man get shot in the chest right outside their doorways. That's a lot of people to not be seeing or hearing a thing."

Shortly after four, the pair returned to the station and found Espinosa in the middle of a chaotic situation involving Scandinavian tourists, prostitutes, and vendors. The confusion had already been raging for an hour and nobody could understand what was going on, because the tourists spoke a language that Espinosa guessed was Swedish or Norwegian and were now trying to explain in English that they had been robbed by the hookers and were demanding the presence of a diplomatic representative of their nation, while the prostitutes were shouting that they didn't know what they were doing there and demanding to know what the faggot foreigners were telling the chief, and the vendors were saying that the foreigners and the hookers had eaten their sandwiches and their beer and refused to pay for them. When he saw Ramiro and Welber arrive, Espinosa handed the case off to the assistant chief and took them into his office to hear what they had to say.

"So, what did you get?"

"Nothing, boss."

"What do you mean, nothing?"

"Nothing. Neither of them saw a thing. If they're telling the truth, the crime occurred just after one-thirty in the morning, when the two cars had already left."

"And were they telling the truth?"

"The styles were different, but in our opinion the architect seemed to be on the defensive," said Ramiro.

"Then let's try one more time. What I think is so strange about this murder is the disproportion between the victim's weakness and the means the criminal used. I think we can eliminate the idea that it was a face-off between two poor homeless people. Neither of them would have a thirty-eight."

"I still think it's possible that some resident or visitor went out to get the car and, upon seeing a one-legged man surge up out of the void at that hour, in the middle of a downpour, imagined they were being robbed and . . ."

". . . and shoots him in the chest," Espinosa completed. "The story makes sense, but the outcome doesn't. Someone who sees a skeletal beggar in the middle of a rainstorm early in the morning might be scared, but they wouldn't start firing away. And it wasn't a bunch of random shots, the startled reaction to a scare, but a single shot, fired precisely into the heart. Whoever shot him knew what he was doing and knew how to shoot. For me, the idea that the shot was fired by someone afraid of being robbed makes as much sense as a shootout between two homeless people—that is, none at all. We don't have anything to go on. Let's keep talking to the residents of the nearby houses, including the people who work at the club. If Skinny, with only one leg, made a point of climbing up that steep street at night and in a downpour, it was because he thought it was worth his trouble. Maybe for some food, maybe for something more. I want you to go back there and get as much information as you can out of those people. You're done for today. Tomorrow morning you can go straight up there."

The chaos created by the tourists, prostitutes, and vendors had died down without anyone having to file an official complaint. They were all let go, after the assistant chief warned the prostitutes and the vendors that if they ever tried to pull anything like that on a day when he was in charge he would throw them in the holding cells until the end of his shift. He furthermore emphasized the point: "You all ought to know that it's designed to hold just one person, so you won't even be able to sit on the ground." When the group left, the decibel level in the area diminished considerably. A few notes were filed on the incident, but nothing suggested that anything else would disturb the peace of the late afternoon.

Espinosa took advantage of the calm to arrange the ideas

floating around his head about the paradoxical figure of Skinny. How could someone so unimportant be the target of such an efficient liquidation? Why would someone worry enough about him that they felt they had to eliminate him? He took a piece of paper, drew a little rectangle in the middle with other rectangles around it, and inside every rectangle wrote a name or placed a question mark; he connected several of the rectangles with lines, and he wrote a few observations underneath. He stared at the paper for a few minutes. Then he took another piece of paper and did the same thing, introducing a few variations. He meticulously examined every one of them, played with more variations, then started examining them all again. After a while, he tore up both sheets of paper and threw them away. He took his gun and his wallet, put on his coat, and went home.

Aldo had arrived home earlier, knowing that Camila wouldn't be there yet. He walked swiftly through their bedroom and the TV room, where Cíntia and Fernando were hypnotized watching a new series, closed the door to shut out the noise, went into the living room, poured himself a little bit of whiskey, sat in the chair that had become his own, and waited for his wife.

He hadn't taken the trouble to open the blinds, so the room was in a quiet semishadow that would have been pleasant if he had been in his normal state. But he wasn't.

He didn't know exactly what he felt. It wasn't a physical discomfort; he was feeling vulnerable. No suffering, no pain, just a vague feeling of vulnerability, which was most likely linked to the visit from the policemen. They had been friendly and polite, they hadn't made any accusations or suggested anything that could be read as a suspicion . . . except, of course, the question about the weapon. Of course it wasn't simple curiosity. The question contained the veiled suggestion that they were looking for people who might have something more to say than just what time exactly they had fetched their cars. It's true that they had to ask about the weapon. After all, a man was killed with a gunshot, and the two cops were looking for the person who had done it, so they couldn't not ask someone who had been at the scene of the crime if he had a weapon. So that's why he was feeling vulnerable. The police had a way of doing that to people, whether they were guilty or not.

He heard Camila's voice speaking to the maid, and then she came into the room.

"Alone in the dark . . . drinking whiskey . . . Problems at work, dear?"

"The police were there."

"The police . . . I know, but isn't that what you told me on the phone, that the police were coming?"

"Sorry. I forgot."

"What did they want?"

"The same thing. About the man killed up at the end of the street."

"And didn't you already tell them what you had to say?"

"They said they just wanted to confirm a few details."

"And did they?"

"I answered their questions. The thing is, they ask questions but always leave a veiled suggestion that you are guilty of something."

"And they're right. We *are* all guilty . . . or at least we all feel guilty. So as far as that goes, they're no different from psychoanalysts or priests. The difference between being guilty and feeling guilty can be very subtle. But of course you didn't come home early from work to sit in the dark with a glass of whiskey, worried, because two cops came on a routine visit."

"Yes, I did."

"How do you mean?"

"I'm worried."

Camila, who until then had been standing beside her husband, sat in a chair across from him and looked into his eyes for a few seconds.

"Why are you so worried, baby? What happened?"

"Nothing. I didn't know what to tell them. They asked me to describe in detail every gesture I made and everything I saw when I got the car. And all I remembered was turning on the engine and going down to get you."

"And isn't that what happened?"

"It is. But what worries me is that I absolutely can't remember anything else. They asked me how I started the car, if my high beams were on or not, if when I turned around the lights picked out anything that I remembered seeing. . . . Anyway, they asked me to describe every second of my time in that cul-de-sac."

"And did you?"

"Yes. But it was all made up."

"Why made up?"

"Because I remember absolutely nothing. I didn't think they'd believe me if I said that."

"But, honey, that doesn't matter. They are going to have to go without a few details that you can't give because you weren't paying attention, and that's it. So there was nothing that grabbed your attention. If they ask you to describe what you saw on the way home from work today, you probably wouldn't be able to remember anything either. They found a beggar shot to death. Once they take note of the occurrence, they have to open an investigation, so that's why they have to find possible witnesses. So since you happened to have your car there in the street, you've become a possible witness. Don't worry, sweetheart—when they realize you have nothing to say, they'll leave you alone."

"Camila, they're not what's bothering me. It's me. It's not the first time this has happened to me."

"This what?"

"This . . . me forgetting . . ."

"Honey, everyone forgets things."

"Camila, if I ask you to describe every step you took and everything you did after you closed your office and came home, you can tell me. I can't manage to say anything about an event so unusual as going out in the middle of a storm to get the car on a dead end street in the middle of the night."

"You'll remember. When you least expect it, you'll remember every detail."

Espinosa got home a little before seven. The maps he'd drawn and torn up when he was leaving the station were still in his head. Since there weren't that many different possibilities, none of them was complex enough to prevent easy memorization. In truth, he wasn't that interested in the possible relations between his two maps, but in the elements themselves. When he thought about them in connection with one another, they didn't resemble anything like a structured whole: it was just a pile of people and facts that didn't seem to have any connection to one another. What did Skinny, a poor homeless man, have to do with the guests at Juliana and Marcos's dinner party? Skinny had something to do with the employees at the club, but even that relationship was fragile, sustained by an old connection with an ex-employee of the club who helped him get leftover food. He continued to get the help after his friend left—which is why he was there at that time. But if that was all, why would anyone kill him?

Seeing the mess that was the product of his weekend with Irene cleared his head completely. His mind was now filled with the image of Irene walking naked through the apartment, when, in fact, at that very moment, she was in São Paulo, probably coming back to the hotel after a day of work. She sometimes stayed no more than a couple of days, but other times she had to stay the whole week, including

Saturday and Sunday. He didn't ask what she did during the week—he guessed that her days were taken up with work—and he didn't ask what she did during the nights and the weekends. Irene, for her part, never asked what Espinosa did during his supposedly solitary days and nights.

He took off his coat, put his weapon and his wallet on the bedside table, and went to see what there was in the refrigerator for dinner. The options were: spaghetti and meatballs and diet lasagna. The only thing worse than that was diet spaghetti, he thought. There was absolutely nothing left from all the things Irene had brought for the weekend. He found a beer at the back of the fridge. Spaghetti and meatballs and beer: that would be his dinner, unless he decided to go out. He put the spaghetti and meatballs in the microwave and walked through the apartment gathering up stray articles of clothing, rearranging furniture and objects that had been displaced during the more animated moments over the course of the weekend. He interrupted the task when he heard the microwave beep. The dinner and the beverage that evening represented the lowest level reached in his recent gastronomy. He would try to make up for it with coffee and by reading a book he'd bought on Friday that was still next to the rocking chair, waiting for a first glance.

He eliminated the traces of his dinner from the kitchen and tried, rather idly, to return the living room to its normal state. He then turned on his reading light, looked at the book as if to say "Stay there, I'll be right back," and went to his bedroom to put on more comfortable clothes.

Back in the living room, seated in the rocking chair that had belonged to his parents, the book on his lap and his eyes staring out at the darkness that the French window, with its little cast-iron balcony, let in, he didn't start to read, or even open the book: turned toward São João Hill, he seemed to be looking for the street where Skinny, who lived on the streets, had been drenched in rainwater after being shot in the chest.

Welber and Ramiro agreed to meet in the Arcoverde subway station, one block from the Rua Mascarenhas de Moraes. They decided to walk up the steep street, in order to get an idea of how much strength Skinny would have had to expend in order to make the same trek with a single leg, crutches, and in the middle of a downpour. They also wanted to see if there was anywhere someone could hide, or whether there were any places where Skinny could have rested on his way up. The first third of the journey left the two panting for breath, and after the first curve, the steepest one, they both began to doubt that the mutilated beggar could have possibly walked up here by himself.

"Don't forget that he went up and down Pavãozinho Hill every day," Welber said.

"Maybe. Don't those Paralympics guys do everything too?"

"Yeah, but they're not poor, malnourished, sick, and weak like Skinny."

"Maybe that's exactly the reason he had to climb up this fucking street late on a rainy night. Or, buddy, maybe it's because there was something good waiting for him at the top."

"There might have been . . . except he couldn't enjoy it."

"Jesus, Welber, they killed the guy."

"And that's bizarre. He was already so fucked up that he hardly even deserved to die. But he was killed with incredible efficiency. A classy job for a victim like that."

They got to the club's gate and went up a little steep walkway perpendicular to the street to the clubhouse. Only the cleaners were working. The only administrative worker on hand had never heard of Skinny and hadn't even heard about the crime that had occurred on the street just outside. The conversation with the two employees got them nowhere, since they only worked during the day.

"The night staff is other people, Chief—we get off at five."

"I'm not a chief. I'm Detective Welber, and the gentleman talking with your colleague is Inspector Ramiro."

"That's fine, Detective, but I've never heard of anyone around here without a leg."

"Skinny."

"What?"

"They called him Skinny."

"Fine. But I don't remember seeing anybody missing a leg here at the club."

"And outside it?"

"I've seen a few, but I don't know who they are."

The conversations with the other employees were equally fruitless. Whatever had brought Skinny up the street with some regularity only happened at night. Unless all the staff were lying, which was improbable, he never came to the club during the day. Welber and Ramiro would have to come back at night.

It wasn't worth going back to the Zona Norte only to have to return at night to interview the other employees. Ramiro and Welber had a long way to go to get home—and what was the point? To sit in the living room waiting for nightfall so they could go back to the club? They went to the station.

Normally fewer people worked at night than during the day, except when the club rented out the pool or the club-house for some private event. When that happened, the number of staff doubled. That wasn't the case this evening. Ramiro and Welber noted the names of the staff members present and each interviewed half of them, a job they finished up just before midnight. Nothing useful was added to what they'd learned in the morning, or what they already knew. The only positive thing was that Skinny, sometimes and very irregularly, appeared when they were cleaning up for the night and asked for some leftover food. He didn't bother anyone and never let himself be seen by any guest of the club; he came in and left by an old path in the side of the hill that could only be accessed by an old stone staircase at the end of the street: five feet from where his body was found.

The next morning Welber and Ramiro phoned Espinosa to tell him what their interviews had uncovered.

"We didn't call you last night because we wanted to speak to the last staff members to leave the club. When we were through with the last interview it was almost midnight, and we thought you might be asleep. . . . Besides the fact that we didn't get anything," said Welber.

"Nothing?"

"Nothing. We talked with all the employees, the cleaners and maintenance people and the cooks and the assistants. We also talked with the administrators. We heard a lot of stories and minute descriptions of their jobs, but nothing that added even the smallest detail to what we already knew about his death. I'd bet my salary that he just went there to get some food, and that was it."

"Good. I want you to send me everything you noted down about him. Once that's done, go to the Forensic Institute and get the best possible picture of the corpse, before they bury him. Get a green shirt to dress him in. I want him to look alive. The picture doesn't have to be of his whole body, just from the waist up. . . . If you can get his eyes open, even better. Then go home and rest. Tomorrow you can go back to the cases you've been working on."

"You're going to shelve it?"

"I am."

"Consider it closed?"

"What do you mean, closed? We didn't even manage to open it."

"And the photo?"

"If they ask, tell them it's in case anyone shows up asking for the body after it's been buried in the paupers' cemetery. That the picture is for recognition."

4

With the sun, the heat of the tropical summer returned after four days of rain and moderate temperatures, along with the prevalence of lighter, less formal clothes for men and women. A few categories of professionals, such as lawyers, continued to walk through downtown in their dark suits and ties, no matter what season it was, a sight that was getting rarer in the Zona Sul and even rarer in Ipanema. The light clothing Aldo wore on his way to work was the same he could have worn to the movies or to dinner with Camila at a local restaurant.

Despite the heat, Aldo decided to walk to work, which meant crossing all of Ipanema down to the Avenida Atlântica. It wasn't so far, three kilometers at the most, but it was extremely hot. He chose the shady side of the street and headed down the Rua Visconde de Pirajá in the direction of the Avenida Atlântica while he thought about the events of the last few days. It wasn't the events of the last few days, actually, just that one day, a night, a part of the night: the moment when he went to get the car. But he had to work, take care of his new projects, help out the interns, and spend more time with Camila. He couldn't waste the whole day thinking about the same thing, obsessing over forgotten details . . . and he knew they were forgotten because the policemen had reminded him of them.

Camila had already seen her first two patients of the afternoon when the door to the waiting room opened to admit Maria.

The waiting room was useless, since no patient ever arrived early, and Camila didn't have anyone to open the door if they had. There was no receptionist, and the patients knew that. The main door was locked until one patient had left, and only then did she admit the next. Camila didn't like to have someone sitting there doing nothing, only waiting to greet the patients. She let the answering machine pick up the phone calls and, depending on how urgent they were, called back during her breaks or at the end of the day. So nobody bothered her, even silently, while she was working.

Maria couldn't make up her mind about how to greet Camila: if, besides saying hello, she sometimes kissed her cheek or shook her hand, sometimes she did neither. Camila waited for her to come in, locked the outside door, and closed the door to the waiting room. The natural light that entered the room was filtered by the blinds, changing according to the time of day. She only turned on the lamp once evening began to fall. As soon as she got there, Maria took off her sandals and lay down on the couch. She wore the usual outfit: T-shirt and shorts, an outfit that, despite its extreme simplicity, was elegant. Sometimes she spent long silent minutes before uttering the first sentence, which was not always a sentence but could be a word, a name; on other occasions she walked in talking, sometimes before she even settled on the couch. But even when that happened, her speech was pleasant and her voice soft. She made it clear that her lack of sexual desire for her husband was not just a matter of not being interested in him—she wasn't interested in men in general. Moreover, it wasn't simply a matter of sexual disinterest: her sexuality could be aroused by something, just not men. That didn't mean that she had started to be sexually attracted to women, though she did find women more interesting than men. And that was the difficulty that led her into analysis: in her opinion, there was nothing wrong with her sexuality, there was something wrong with other people. . . . Not exactly wrong, she had said; it wasn't about being wrong or right . . . people were stereotypical, poor, boring.

This afternoon she was chatty, and the tone and soft musicality of her voice were pleasant for Camila. There was still the movement of her feet . . . softer that afternoon, since she was speaking more . . . and then the gesturing hands . . . and the hair . . . black, shiny, full . . . swinging from one side to the other when she moved her head. In the previous session, Camila had experimented with taking a bit of her hair between her thumb and index finger. Nothing Maria had noticed. And there it was, once again, that full, dense, hair, spilling onto the side of the sofa, within reach, even without Camila having to stretch out her arm. At that moment, Maria was silent, only her feet speaking to each other. Camila moved her hand and closed it over a considerable quantity of hair, more than the minimum necessary to be perceived by Maria. Maria didn't move her head and she didn't say a word . . . and so they remained for a time, as if waiting for something, Maria never showing that she had noticed Camila's gesture, but immobile enough to let the analyst know that the ball was still in her court. Camila softly stroked the hair. Maria, without turning around, reached back and put her hand on Camila's.

In the elevator, before he even opened the door of his office, Aldo was sure that he would find the cops there waiting for him. He hadn't said anything to Mercedes, his architect colleague, or to Rafaela and Henrique, the interns. The policemen could have arrived saying that they had an appointment with Aldo Bruno and been invited to come in. Or they could have left a message saying they'd be over before noon. He opened the door suddenly to surprise them. They weren't there. He gathered his little group around him to discuss meeting all the deadlines for their latest project. They stopped at twelve-thirty for lunch.

"Is there a problem?" asked Mercedes when the interns were otherwise occupied.

"No. Why?"

"Because there's obviously something bothering you. It might be personal, in which case I won't get involved, but if it's something about work, I might be able to help."

"It's not about my family . . . it's not work. . . . It's personal. . . . And I don't even know if it's a problem, because I can't quite say what it is. . . . It's very simple. . . . I'm having blackouts in my memory."

"That happens to everyone—what's the problem?"

"The problem is that when it happens to me, the problem starts haunting me."

"Do you want to talk about it while we eat? What about Japanese?"

"Thanks. Let's go."

Mercedes was twenty years younger than Aldo. His assistant, a good worker, pretty . . . some things brought them together, while others kept them apart. Aldo knew how careful he had to be to keep order in the office. Mercedes had been born in Argentina, the daughter of an Argentine mother and a Brazilian father. She was bilingual, but she had a distant and charming Buenos Aires lilt in her voice. They often ate together, all four of them, though more often Mercedes, Rafaela, and Henrique went out earlier and Aldo waited for them to come back before going out alone. It was less common but not rare for Aldo and Mercedes to go out together. The restaurants on their block offered a choice between Italian, Portuguese, Chinese, and Japanese, as well as a buffet of undefined nationality. They could eat at a different place every day, but they tended to hover between the Italian and the Japanese.

As soon as they had ordered, Mercedes resumed the conversation.

"What do you mean you're forgetting . . . blacking out, as you said."

"It's exactly that: blacking out."

"All the time? Several times a day?"

"No. That's not it, since I wouldn't be able to work. It's not every day . . . but it happens."

"When was the last time?"

"Thursday night."

"And what happened?"

"The bad thing is that it involves the police. I had to lie to hide the fact that I didn't remember anything."

At the mention of the police, Mercedes's expression changed. Aldo told her about getting the car after the dinner, and how he had completely forgotten what had happened immediately thereafter. He also explained why the police had been interested in interviewing him in the first place.

"It could have happened exactly as you said: you were running through the rain, jumped into the car to get out of the rain, started the car, and drove down to the door of the house. If there was a cadaver stretched out in the middle of the street, you would have seen it. If you didn't see anything—and that's why you don't remember anything— it's because there was no cadaver stretched out in the middle of the street. And that's it. What's the problem?"

"The problem is that I made up a story full of details to hide what I ought to have seen and remembered the next day."

"Can you remember everything you saw last night? Or even this morning, ever since you walked out of your door?"

"That's what I keep trying to tell myself. But I can't be convinced. It's one thing not to remember the millions of details of my morning walk to the office, and another thing not to be able to remember a very specific scene, a square, the end of a street, no more than ten meters across."

"I don't know why it's bothering you so much. Have there been other incidents?"

"With the police?"

"No, with forgetting things . . ."

"A few, but this is the one that's tormenting me."

The sushi-sashimi combos arrived and a silence fell between them. Aldo tried to see what effect his story had had on Mercedes, but she was completely focused on the food. That was characteristic of her; she could concentrate on different things without being flighty. After examining the pieces on her plate, unwrapping and separating the parts of the sushi, and tasting the first sashimi, she turned to Aldo as if the conversation had never stopped.

"And is that really what's bothering you?"

"What do you mean?"

"This forgetfulness . . . is there nothing else connected to it?"

"How can I know?"

"It's not by chance that it happened to you on a dead-end street . . ."

Mercedes put down her chopsticks and placed her hand on Aldo's.

"Maybe it's not the best time or the best place for us to

talk about this. Why don't we finish our lunch and walk down the Avenida Atlântica—on the shady side, of course—and talk about it there?"

The restaurant was on a street perpendicular to the beach, so they walked naturally toward their destination. The office was in a building halfway down the block; they could walk a couple of blocks or go in as soon as they reached the entrance. They went in. Alone in the elevator, they silently followed the lights that lit up the numbers of the floors until they arrived.

Over the course of the afternoon, Aldo once again assembled his team to continue that morning's discussion. He assigned individual tasks to each of the interns and tried to act as naturally as possible with Mercedes. That was the hardest part, given the kinds of things she had pointed out at lunch, along with the explicit suggestion that came with taking his hand and suggesting they continue the conversation somewhere else. "This forgetfulness," she had said, "is there nothing else connected to it?" Of course there was, damn it! he thought. So what? The only thing the cops told the people they interviewed was that a man had been killed. Obviously shot, Aldo reflected; otherwise they wouldn't have asked me if I had a revolver. . . . By the way, I had a revolver . . . and that's the other question: What happened to the revolver? I remember it perfectly, a Taurus .38, but I can't remember what happened to it. Just to be safe, I told the police that my revolver was a .32, and that I'd given it up during a disarmament campaign. Why all the lies?

Mercedes, Rafaela, and Henrique had gone home. Night had fallen. The lights on the Avenida Atlântica had come on and there was intense traffic heading toward Ipanema and Leblon. For the first time he didn't want to be in the office alone . . . especially at night. He went downstairs and got a taxi to take him home.

Camila was already there, eating dinner with the kids. He was simultaneously greeted by all three, two of whom had their mouths full. He joined them and listened to the stories they were telling about their days, which forced him to look from one to the other attentively, as if watching a Ping-Pong match. After the dinner and the stories, the two kids got up, Fernando heading for his video games and Cíntia for the phone.

Aldo took Camila's hand and led her into the living room. He told her how he was feeling about his forgetfulness and the lies he'd told the police.

"Why did I lie, Camila?"

"Because you are fully aware of the lacuna in your memory, so you feel forced to fill it up. The difference is that in this case the filling is deliberately false—your objective is only to fool the other, the policeman, but not yourself. Have you forgotten other things? Do you forget people's names, do you forget meetings, to pay your bills, that kind of thing?"

"No."

"So then."

"So then what?"

"Then your memory is fine.... It's been affected by some external factor.... You just can't remember what happened during a specific moment in time. You still can't remember anything? Not even a little detail?"

"The only thing I can remember when I try to go back to that moment is the image of an old wooden gate ... and my going through that gate."

"Do you know what gate it is?"

"No."

"Is there a gate up on that street?"

"I don't know. I could even go there tomorrow to see. Camila ... another thing ..."

"What, sweetheart?"

"What happened to my revolver?"

"It must be hidden in your closet ... in a drawer ... on a high shelf ..."

"I already looked in all those places. I'm sure it's not here in the house."

"Couldn't it be in the glove compartment? You put it there a few times ... when we went on trips, or went out late at night."

Wednesday. A nice morning, not too hot. Mood, none too great. Espinosa took the shortest route to work. The shortest and the least attractive. The most attractive went down the Rua Barata Ribeiro, especially when he had time to go through the shelves and stands of the secondhand bookstore in the hopes of finding a good book, or through the Galeria Menescal, where he was drawn to the meatballs sold at the Arab restaurant. Taking the least attractive route meant not being interested in the landscape, in the people, in the movement on the street—it meant being completely focused on his own ideas, which in general were not very pleasant on these bad-mood mornings. It didn't matter that it was Wednesday, two days before a possible meeting with Irene, because it was a Wednesday that had followed a Tuesday in which he had been forced to shelve a case that had only a remote chance of being resolved satisfactorily, because he couldn't spare two of his most competent colleagues to investigate the death of a man whose invisibility matched his murderer's. The victim had no official existence, his name was nothing more than a nickname, he had no documents, residence, family, friends, acquaintances, or circle of relations, no matter how flimsy. He was homeless, identity-less, family-less. . . . His poverty was such that the only thing that identified him was a negative: the lack of a leg.

The walk to work wasn't long enough for Espinosa to think through the situation, though he always said he didn't so much think as let his ideas flow freely. So it was a shock when he arrived in his office and found on the table a photo of Skinny looking straight into the camera, defying the photographer.

"So, Chief, what do you think?" It was Ramiro, coming into the room followed by Welber.

"How did you pull it off?"

"The work of our detective-photographer Welber."

"Excellent."

"Half the credit goes to the staff of the Forensic Institute. They were great," said Welber. "The other half of the
credit belongs to you. All we had to do was say it was your
request and everyone helped out. The third half belongs to
my cell phone, because the only camera we had was on it;
finally, the last half of the credit belongs to the computer,
which retouched the picture and opened Skinny's eyes, and
also put him square on his feet. It was the best we could do.
Since none of us saw him with his eyes open, we can't com-
pare. But . . . here's the dead guy . . . alive."

"Fantastic."

"Now that we've done it, can you tell us what you plan to
do with the picture?"

"Show it to the murderer."

Of course, Espinosa didn't know who the murderer was.
He didn't even have any suspects. He just had a few possibilities, and even those were highly improbable. He considered anyone who could have gotten to Skinny that night,
under the downpour, a possibility—people who could have
come up the street, on foot or in a car, or people who were
already up there. Nobody was seen coming up the street,
except one person in a car and another in a taxi. It was
unlikely that someone would have gone up the street in a
taxi in order to murder a homeless person. The most probable thing, therefore, was that the murderer was already
nearby. If it was some resident of the building, the doorman

would have seen him or her enter and depart. So other possibilities, improbable though they might be, were the guests at the dinner party in the new house. Among them, only two had parked at the end of the street. So no matter how improbable they seemed, Espinosa was going to show them the picture. The important thing was to take them by surprise. It would be a unique opportunity for the chief to observe their reactions. If they were caught off guard, or if they suspected what they were about to see, there wouldn't be a second chance.

Thanks to Photoshop, the picture showed Skinny wearing a normal shirt, shorts, and sandals, standing up, leaning into his crutches. The background was dark and undefined and could have been a stone wall, and the man looked fixedly into the camera as if surprised by the photographer. The amazing resurrection of the dead man was the work of Ramiro's teenage nephew, whose main source of entertainment was composing embarrassing scenes in which some public figure appeared at a bacchanal, or creating images of a person by borrowing parts of others. The kid had had no trouble creating the picture.

On Thursday morning, Espinosa called Rogério Antunes and Aldo Bruno to make appointments with each of them. "It'll be quick," he promised. "I won't take more than ten minutes of your time." Neither was very receptive, but they both agreed to allow him ten minutes that afternoon. Because of the impression of the two men Welber and Ramiro had given him, Espinosa chose to interview Rogério Antunes first. Once again, they met on the veranda of the

Yacht Club, which appeared to function as the young executive's office. It certainly had a nice view.

"A pleasure to meet you personally, sir."

"The pleasure is all mine, Officer. I've already had the opportunity to meet your colleagues, who were very nice. We had a nice conversation, though unfortunately I couldn't help much. In fact, I don't think I helped at all."

"Sometimes not being able to help is a big help."

"Well, Chief, did anything new turn up? Maybe I can be more helpful this time . . ."

"Thank you, sir. Actually, something turned up that might be a promising track. . . . A suspect . . . he was identified by the doorman of one of the nearby buildings."

Espinosa took the picture out of his jacket pocket and placed it on the table. Rogério Antunes looked at it, picked it up, and examined it in more detail.

"This is the suspect? He doesn't have a leg. . . . He looks like a poor guy."

"You've never seen this man?"

"Never, sir. Who is it?"

"Nobody knows for sure. . . . Thanks so much. Once again, your help is appreciated." Espinosa took the photo and replaced it in his pocket.

"But I didn't help at all."

"Exactly, Mr. Antunes. Once again, thank you. See you around. Beautiful view you've got here."

He slipped into a cab that had just dropped someone off at the club and headed for the Avenida Atlântica, where he would meet Aldo Bruno.

Mercedes opened the door, which made Espinosa forget the view from the Yacht Club.

"Good afternoon. You must be Chief Espinosa. Aldo said you'd be coming. He's in the other room. . . . Come in, please."

Espinosa had not yet completely absorbed the intimacy in the phrase "Aldo said" when he was introduced to the two interns and then led to Aldo Bruno's office. In the office, there was a large drafting table, an old-style one that could be adjusted with pedals, and a table with the biggest computer screen Espinosa had ever seen. The architect got up to greet the chief.

"Sir, pleasure to meet you. Please, have a seat. You said over the phone that something had come up and that you needed my help."

"That's right. A suspect was positively identified by the doorman of a neighboring building. There are strong signs that he committed the crime."

With a studied gesture, Espinosa took the picture from his pocket and handed it to the architect. Aldo looked at it.

"But this . . ."

"This . . . ?"

Aldo handed the photo back to Espinosa as if it were contaminated.

". . . is a man missing a leg."

"Without a leg, but with two arms he could fire a weapon."

"Is he the one who did?"

"Everything indicates that he was. Did you see this

man at the end of the street or on the street itself or any-where else?"

"No. Certainly not. I would remember . . . because of the leg."

"Thanks, Mr. Bruno. The ten minutes I requested are already up; I don't want to take more of your time."

Aldo walked Espinosa to the door, said good-bye, and closed the door. Espinosa could hardly contain himself—the architect could be watching through the peephole—until he was inside the elevator; there he dropped the indifferent expression with which he had said farewell to Aldo Bruno. The architect had certainly recognized Skinny. "But this . . ." He had said everything but the name. The elevator reached the ground floor and Espinosa left the building, stepping onto the sidewalk, but instead of hailing a taxi he opted to walk along the Avenida Atlântica toward the station. It was a long walk, but the view made up for it. Besides, he needed to mull over what had just happened, and he could think better while walking.

He hadn't expected the picture to bear fruit so quickly. Aldo Bruno had recognized Skinny. The fear in his reaction had been more than obvious—it had been shocking. The architect was truly affected, and only a miracle had kept him from saying the homeless man's name. A double shock: that the "suspect" was Skinny, and that Skinny was still alive. And the conclusion that Espinosa had to make from the shock and the fear: that Aldo was the murderer. Or, in the best-case scenario, had witnessed the murder.

That much was clear. It just didn't make sense.

Why would a young, good-looking, rich, happily married, professionally successful man risk it all by murdering a poor and apparently inoffensive homeless man? It hadn't been an accidental death. The murder hadn't been unintentional. Skinny was killed by a shot to the chest, not accidentally run over by a car on a dark and rainy night. Why? Espinosa imagined the architect arriving at the house with his pretty wife (Espinosa imagined that she was pretty) for a dinner celebrating the inauguration of a house he had done, where he was introduced to the owners' friends. The dinner party goes perfectly, everyone is lovely, the food is delicious, the conversation is pleasant and punctuated with exclamations over the new house. After the dinner, the architect leaves his wife waiting in front of the house, runs to the end of the street, fifty meters away, to get the car. He gets in, starts the engine and turns on the lights; at that moment he sees Skinny standing there, in the rain, leaning into his crutches, a few feet away, in the dark, trying to signal his presence to the driver. The architect opens the glove compartment, takes out a revolver, gets out of the car, aims at the man's chest, and fires.

The story made no sense at all.

He walked the rest of the way to the station trying to come up with variations on the story based on the information Ramiro and Welber had gathered from the other participants in the dinner and the employees of the house. Nothing could account for the tragic events of the night.

It meant nothing that Aldo Bruno had recognized Skinny if there was nothing to connect the two.

Aldo said he was alone when he fetched the car . . . that he had left his wife waiting in the doorway of the house because of the rain . . . that he had driven the car back around and picked up his wife . . . Camila Pontes Bruno. Espinosa thought it was time to meet Dr. Camila. He looked at the list of guests at the dinner and found only her home number. He called, and the maid gave him the number of her office. He called the new number and left a message asking her to call before seven that evening or the next day.

When he left the station at seven-fifteen, Camila Bruno still hadn't called.

Antonia had never bothered to say how old she was, but Camila estimated she was between twenty-five and thirty. The only thing she had said on the very first day was that she'd been born in Portugal and had spent five years of her childhood in Argentina. She'd gone to high school in Lisbon and came to Brazil intending to study architecture, but after she graduated she became interested in the Portuguese architecture of Brazil and decided to obtain a master's in Portuguese colonial history. She told Camila this to justify the light Portuguese accent she still had after ten years in Brazil. Camila loved her accent. The only thing Antonia had in common with Maria (besides the fact that Antonia was formally named Maria Antonia) was her black hair, Maria's long and wavy, Antonia's short, voluminous, and smooth . . . as well as the discreet sensuality, almost shy but powerful—Camila had no doubt about it. If it were up to her, she would have only female patients; she thought her male patients were unbelievably monotonous. The comparison with Maria was involuntary, the image of one appearing whenever she was in the presence of the other. And there was Antonia stretched out on her couch, still silent, as if waiting to see what would come out at the beginning of that session.

Antonia was less informal in her dress, her gestures were more contained, and she didn't take off her shoes when she stretched out on the couch. Of the few movements she made during the session, Camila still couldn't tell if one in particular was intentional—or, at least, consciously intentional: she almost always wore shirts that buttoned in the front without a bra, and one of her repeated gestures was to cross her hands behind her head, at which point the blouse, whose upper buttons weren't fastened, exposed almost the entirety of one of her breasts. It might have been the casual attitude of one woman with another, but it might also have been a seductive game played by a woman who knew she was discreetly provoking.

Camila's first attempts to get closer to her came through interpretation, and her patient met those forays with silence. That silence was common with Antonia; more than once she'd sat through an entire session without saying a single word. But the silence that day was different; there was something in it that was a bit provocative. . . . Or at least

Camila wanted it to be. She risked a touch on her patient's arm as she spoke to her. There was no reaction, either of surprise or of moving away . . . the arm stayed in the same position. Then she risked placing her hand on Antonia's arm. The arm relaxed and the patient's breath accelerated slightly, exposing her breast entirely. Camila softly moved her hand down Antonia's arm. The next patient, the last of the day, had called the night before to say he couldn't make it.

The afternoon would have been perfect if not for the policeman's message on the answering machine. Not content with speaking to Aldo, he now wanted to meet with her. She would call the next day, after she'd spoken with her husband.

Aldo arrived home later than usual. The kids were already in bed and Camila was waiting for him for dinner. Before he said anything, she knew, by the way he opened the door and came into the room, that something had happened. And it wasn't something good.

"Sorry, honey, I got stuck at the office . . ."

"I was worried—you usually call."

"It was a last-minute thing . . ."

"Okay. Let's eat and forget about it . . . at least while we're eating."

The dinner started with slow movements on Aldo's part, accompanied by pauses, almost stutters, in his speech. Camila placed the silverware on the table and sat looking at her husband while she waited for him to resume his normal behavior. But that didn't happen.

"Sweetheart, what was the last-minute problem? Was there really a last-minute problem?"

"Yes . . . no . . ."

"Yes or no?"

"There was, but I don't think it was last-minute."

"Was it something to do with Chief Espinosa?"

"How did you know?"

"He called me. He left a message, but I'm going to call him back tomorrow—I wanted to talk to you first. Did he come see you at the office?"

"He did. Just for a couple of minutes. He just wanted to show me the picture of the suspect . . . who killed the homeless man."

"And? You didn't happen to recognize him?"

"I did."

"You did? How? Was it someone at the dinner party?"

"No."

"Then who was it?"

"I still don't know. . . . I'm confused. . . . I think I'm mixing things up."

"What are you mixing up, honey?"

"Things . . . the days. . . . I'm very confused. He can't have been the suspect."

"Who can't be a suspect? The man in the picture?"

"Yeah."

"Why?"

"Because he died, Camila."

"He died? Did you know him?"

"He was the dead man who was found at the end of that street."

"How can you know that?"

"I'm very tired. . . . I want to sleep."

Friday, ten A.M.

"Chief, a call for you. Camila Bruno."

Espinosa knew she'd call only after talking with her husband and, possibly, with her lawyer.

"Dr. Camila, good morning. . . . Thanks for calling."

"Good morning. You're Chief Espinosa?"

"That's right. I left a message for you last night."

"I wanted to talk to my husband before calling you back."

"That's fine. I'd like to talk to you for a few minutes. But I'd like it to be personally."

"We are speaking personally, sir."

"Not entirely, ma'am. If you don't mind, I'd like to speak face-to-face. You, as much as anyone, can understand why."

"Yes, I understand."

"It can be before lunch . . . or even during lunch, if you're booked."

"It can be before lunch—I don't have any appointments this morning."

"Great. Is eleven all right?"

"Fine. But I'd rather meet in my office, not at home."

Espinosa noted the address and checked the time. He had an hour. If he took a cab, he'd have forty minutes to visit one of his favorite bookstores, on the same block as Camila's office.

Camila was a bit annoyed by having to change her gym hour, but she was curious to know what the detective wanted. Aldo had promised that he was a polite man. That's why she felt comfortable seeing him in her office. She got there a half hour early. She wanted time to get organized. At eleven on the dot she opened the door after hearing the bell.

It was a surprise. For both of them, as far as she could tell. A man stood before her who was the same age as Aldo, wearing an untucked short-sleeved shirt and carrying a bag of books from the bookstore she'd visited for years.

"Chief Espinosa?"

"Dr. Camila?"

Besides the analyst's chair and the couch, the office also had another chair, which Camila used during interviews, and where she invited Espinosa to sit. The spacious room, with a nice bookshelf along one side and a nice view of the lagoon behind the low buildings of Ipanema, pleased Espinosa.

"So, Officer, we seem to frequent the same bookstore," Camila said, indicating with a glance the bag that Espinosa had placed on the table next to the chair.

"Only very occasionally. I rarely come to Ipanema, since my precinct is in Copacabana, and for me it's easier to get in the subway and go to the bookstores downtown."

"So you only come to Ipanema when it's an important matter?"

"I think so . . . though the criteria for importance can vary. It can be a visit to a bookshop or a professional interview. Thank you for agreeing to see me so quickly."

"How can I help you?"

"By telling me what happened on the night last week when you and your husband went to dinner at the top of the Rua Mascarenhas de Moraes. I'm not interested in the dinner itself, but in what happened when you left."

"Nothing. It was raining, my husband went to get the car, which was parked nearby, and we went home."

"Do you know where the car was parked?"

"At the end of the street . . . a short distance from the house. . . . It's a dead-end street."

"Did you go with him to get the car?"

"No. It was raining hard, we didn't have an umbrella, and Aldo said he'd run over to the car. I waited inside the door."

"Did it take him a long time to get the car?"

"No. Just a second. The time to get there, turn around, and come back. Hard to say . . . five minutes, ten minutes at most."

"Did you hear anything during the time he was gone?"

"It was raining really hard, banging, thundering . . ."

"When he came back, did you notice anything different? Was he nervous, anxious . . . ?"

"I didn't notice anything. Both of us were tired, he was

maneuvering down the hill, since that street is so narrow and steep, and the windshield wipers could hardly keep up with the pouring rain . . ."

"Does your husband usually have a weapon with him or in the glove compartment when you go out at night?"

"Aldo doesn't have a gun, if you're trying to figure out if he fired at that man. . . . Because that is obviously the connection you're trying to establish between him having gone to get the car and the man who was found dead."

"You're right. That's the nexus I'm trying to establish—or eliminate once and for all. My questions might seem impertinent, but they can just as easily be in someone's favor as to their detriment."

"Are you really thinking my husband killed that homeless man?"

"No. I'm just gathering information from the only people who were at the scene of the crime around the time it was committed. There's no doubt the murderer was there. It wasn't a suicide. That your husband and Rogério Antunes were there, there's also no doubt, they've said so themselves. Besides that, I don't have anything. That's why I keep asking. I'm trying to collect any information that could be useful in determining who committed the crime."

"But if you are asking if my husband has a gun in his glove compartment, it's because you think he is a possible suspect."

"Not necessarily. If he had a gun in his glove compartment it could have been stolen during the dinner and used for the crime. It's very common for cars parked in dark places to be broken into and looted."

"But that's not what happened to our car, I don't think."

"Apparently not. Your husband made no reference to that. But if you say that he doesn't have a firearm . . ."

"And he must have said the same thing when you talked to him."

"That's true. He said something about a disarmament campaign . . . years ago. . . . He turned it in to be destroyed."

"Then your question's been answered, I think."

"I think so too. So, Dr. Camila, all I can do is thank you for agreeing to see me on such short notice. Sorry for taking your time. Your office is done with beautiful taste, and the same for your library. It must be nice to work in a place like this . . . as long as impertinent policemen don't disturb your peace, of course."

They both got up at the same time. On the way to the door, Espinosa pulled a piece of paper out of the bag of books, unfolded it, and showed it to Camila.

"One more thing, Doctor. Have you ever seen this man?"

She took the paper and scrutinized the picture.

"No. Never. Strange, that picture."

"You're right, it's not very good. The copy was made on bad paper."

"That's not it. The man looks strange . . . like a doll."

"You're a bit right about that."

"Anyway, I can guarantee I've never seen this man."

"Thanks once again. See you."

Back in the street, he looked at the sky. Matisse blue, he thought. And he thought about what he had thought. No other police chief went to interview witnesses after stopping off at the best bookstore in the neighborhood and selecting three books—Faulkner, Coetzee, and Patricia Highsmith—did the interview and got enraptured by the beauty of the interviewee, and then went out into the street, looked at the sky, and thought "Matisse blue." Something was wrong with this picture. It didn't match the person . . . or the screenplay was all right and the director was no good. But it wasn't a film or a play, it was real life, and the character was not played by an artist but was himself: Espinosa, a police chief who had never seen a Matisse in real life. He kept walking and thinking about what a strange person he was. Not strange, exactly. "Eccentric" was a better term . . . or "off-key." Eccentric, off-key, in relation to the police. But nobody spends twenty years in one institution, occupying important positions, and remains eccentric, out of line with the same institution. Unless, of course, he's an idiot. Besides being strange or eccentric, he was also an idiot. Which was not too far from the truth, if the word "idiot" can apply to a person turned in on himself, his own questions, his own world. That was a better way of putting it: he lived in his own world.

He was hungry. Not exactly hungry, but it was lunchtime. Pure habit. Except that he wasn't at the station, he was outside, in Ipanema, at the end of Ipanema, almost in Leblon. . . . He could take advantage of the different neighborhood to try something out of the usual circle of McDonald's, trattoria, bar, roast chicken. He looked at his watch. Almost noon. There were lots of small, nice restaurants on the very block where he was walking. And they were still empty, though they would fill up in fifteen minutes. He chose one that seemed to be appropriate to his mood and asked for a house salad. A few minutes later he knew he'd chosen the right thing. It was a delicious change from his police routine. It would last an hour or maybe a bit longer, if he stretched out as long as he could a large salad accompanied by a chicken breast. Once the detour was over, he would go back to the station. After lunch, he allowed himself another half hour to examine the shops in the neighborhood and the people who walked down the elegant sidewalks, a different group than he was used to seeing in Copacabana.

When he got back to the station, he found two messages: one from Irene, saying that she'd be in Rio for the weekend, and the other from Rogério Antunes, leaving his office and cell numbers, asking for him to call back.

He called Rogério first. At that hour, he would still be at lunch, almost certainly at the Yacht Club.

"Officer, thank you for returning my call. It's a bit awkward. . . . I didn't tell you everything I ought to have said. . . . I hope you'll excuse me . . ."

"You saw the body."

"I did."

"Why didn't you tell me the truth when we spoke?"

"Because I didn't want to get involved in a police investigation. Especially when it was a matter of homicide."

"And how do you know that it's a matter of homicide?"

"After you asked to speak with me personally, I didn't have any question that something serious had happened, and when I called my friend and he said that the police had asked for a list of the guests at the dinner party, I no longer had any doubt. Someone had been killed. I also learned that the victim was a beggar. I didn't think the investigation would go on much longer."

"And so, in order not to ruin your day, you decided not to say that you'd seen a body in the street."

"I'm sorry, sir. That's why I called you: to make good on the mistake."

"Or because you're afraid of being incriminated, after you found out the other people at the dinner party were also being interviewed."

The first patient that afternoon was Maria, which always brought Camila a foretaste of pleasure. She regretted that the officer's visit had ruined a bit of her day. He was an interesting figure, the officer—it was a shame he was from the police. If he did something else it would be a different situation. Or was she interested in him precisely because he was a police chief? Dangerous job: shoot-outs with bandits, guns . . . it all added a certain spice. But she didn't like cops, though she thought the detective-philosopher was interesting and attractive. Nevertheless, the promise of the afternoon, and the nature of the session was already hinted at by the way Maria arrived. When Camila opened the door to her, Maria kissed her on the corner of her mouth, and as soon as the door was locked she kicked off her sandals and dropped her purse on the floor.

There were two reasons why Espinosa preferred to have Irene come to his apartment in the Peixoto District rather than going to her place in Ipanema. First, he thought his apartment was more relaxing, less formal, without the immaculately white carpets and sofas, without the works of art spread out on the tables and the paintings on the walls. The fact is, they behaved themselves more in her apartment. The second thing was that ever since some criminals had threatened to kidnap Irene in order to put pressure on him, Espinosa didn't want her address to be widely known. But that afternoon he suggested exactly the opposite: that they spend the weekend in Ipanema, or even in a hotel.

"Why, babe? Did something happen in your apartment?"

"I'm being invaded, and I had to take drastic measures."

"Invaded by whom?"

"Not by whom, by what. Little ants . . . tiny little ants . . . if such a thing is possible: ants are already tiny, so talking about tiny ants is kind of like talking about big elephants, redundant . . ."

"*Sí, pero no es lo mismo.* It's not the same. Imagine your apartment being invaded by elephants."

"Irene, I'm serious."

"But what are these incredible ants doing?"

"Walking around! In lines! They only walk in lines,

except one, who walks along the line in the opposite direction, giving orders and directions!"

"But, honey, you're leaving your house because of tiny little ants? And such polite ones, too. . . . If they were fire ants I'd understand, but little bitty ones . . ."

"Irene, there's a lot of them! They're on the walls of the living room, in the kitchen sink, crossing the bathroom floor, in the hall, on the balcony . . ."

"Fine—except for the living room walls they're in places where we've been known to make love, and I understand that you don't want the ants crawling over your butt, or mine. Get your stuff and come over."

That was what Espinosa was about to do, when the phone rang.

"Chief Espinosa."

"Chief, this is Aldo Bruno."

"Yes, Mr. Bruno, how can I help you?"

"I need to speak with you."

"Yes . . ."

"I'd like to do so personally. I'm in my office—I can get in a cab and be there in ten minutes."

"I'm about to leave. I have an appointment in a few minutes. I can wait for you to get here and then we can walk to the Peixoto District, where I live. We can talk along the way."

"Fine. I'll meet you in ten or fifteen minutes in front of the station."

Espinosa had suspected that something like this was about to happen, but he'd thought he would have to wait

until next week. Instead it had happened in the last few
minutes before he was about to leave for Irene's apartment,
from where he wouldn't return until Sunday night. He left
a written note for Welber and Ramiro, turned off his computer, gave a few instructions to the cops on duty, and went
downstairs to await the architect, who really did arrive
within the fifteen minutes Espinosa had allotted. He waited
for Bruno to pay the taxi driver and walked over.

"How are you, Mr. Bruno?"

"Not very well, Officer."

"Shall we walk? That way you can tell me what's
going on."

"I wish that dinner had never happened."

"But it did."

"Unfortunately . . . and something else happened that I
didn't tell you about and that's been tormenting me."

"Yes?"

"I didn't tell you the truth when you were in my office. I
saw the man's body in the street when I went to get the car."

"Where was it?"

"It was on the cobblestones, near the stone wall. I saw it
even before I got in the car. I turned on the lights and went
to look closer. . . . That's when I saw the bloodstain on his
chest, a little bit washed off by the rain. He was obviously
dead. That's when I realized the murderer could still be
around . . . he could think that I saw the crime and kill me
as well. . . . I ran back to the car and picked up my wife. It
all happened in a flash."

"Why didn't you tell me the truth when we talked?"

"Out of fear."

"Fear of what?"

"I don't know. . . . Fear . . . just fear. I couldn't understand how the man I had seen dead on the street could be in that picture, alive, looking at the camera. When you showed me the photo, I was so shocked that I almost said that he was the man I'd seen dead. And I still don't understand."

"Photoshop."

"I should have thought of that. I was still bothered by the whole thing . . . especially because of the lie I told you."

"So why did you decide to tell me now?"

"Because Rogério Antunes, who had also parked up in the cul-de-sac, called me to tell me about the conversation you'd had with him. When he said he'd also seen the body—which I thought hadn't happened, because his car was already pointing down the hill—I realized you would know I was lying. Which was confirmed when my wife told me you wanted to speak with her personally."

They were crossing the Praça Edmundo Bittencourt, the heart of the Peixoto District, and paused beside a stone bench. There was still a bit of daylight when the streetlights came on. The two men were looking at each other when Espinosa spoke.

"Mr. Bruno, when we spoke yesterday, as when you spoke with my assistants, Inspector Ramiro and Detective Welber, they were informal conversations, though they were informative. You weren't giving an official deposition and you weren't under oath. That informality ends today.

In fact, it's ending right now. From now on, I suggest that you—and the same goes for Rogério Antunes or anybody else we've been talking to—tell the truth. I won't worry about what you've previously told me. I'm not doing this because I have a good heart. I don't. I'm doing this because you two are the only witnesses I've got. For now."

"My wife didn't . . ."

"Dr. Camila didn't say anything to compromise you or herself. Now if you'll excuse me. I said I had an appointment."

He waited for the architect to walk off before he headed to his building. He walked up the stairs to the third floor, went in, turned on all the lights, and examined all the rooms. Then he picked up the phone.

"Irene."

"Hey, hon, something come up?"

"The ants are gone."

"How do you mean? You killed the poor things?"

"No, they just disappeared. There's not a single one left. I didn't spray and I didn't call the exterminators. Irene, they're like an occupying army, and since they can't occupy the whole thing all the time, they occupy a building here and an apartment there. . . . Then they're off to occupy other apartments and buildings."

"And why do they do it?"

"To occupy them, of course!"

"To do what with them?"

"Irene, don't you understand? Occupation isn't a means, it's an end. Once it's occupied, that's it. It's over."

"Espinosa, dear, I think you're going insane. Instead of you coming over here, I'll come over there. I'm afraid to let you walk the streets alone."

"So you're coming?"

"Of course. You're usually interesting, but crazy ... ."

Despite the last-minute change of plans, Irene arrived in her usual good humor, and with her usual two bags of wine, bread, cheese, and cold cuts. Pausing in the doorway, she gently put down the bags and, ignoring Espinosa, who was standing up and waiting for her with outstretched arms, cast an inquisitive glance inside.

"The hordes . . . they haven't returned?"

"No, they capitulated when they heard you were on the way. They beat a retreat, shouting, 'Irene's coming!'"

"Espinosa, tell me something. Were there really ants in this apartment?"

"Tons."

"I don't believe a word of it. I think you make up these stories when you're alone, a kind of tryout for when you decide to sit down and write fiction. Confess: Were there really any ants?"

"A few . . . in the kitchen . . . but all lined up!"

An hour later, a bottle of wine had vanished, along with lots of cheese and meat, and they were stretched out on the living room sofa with their legs wrapped around each other's. Espinosa summed up the case of the homeless man for Irene.

"So why did you get involved personally in this case? Why didn't you let your underlings take care of it? Saturday you said it reminded you of something from your childhood. Is that the reason?"

"The scene of the crime is the end of a street just a few blocks away from here. It's a very steep street, and when I was a kid we called it Otto's Street, which for us, mounted on our bicycles, represented the maximum of daring and exploring new lands. I say 'our' because there were five of us who were around thirteen years old, discovering the world. . . . And exactly the place where the homeless man was murdered was the high point of our adventure, our secret place. At that time there was no construction there: you could see all of Copacabana. Whenever I think of the scene of the crime, I think of the scene of my childhood. But there's also the absurd fact of an obviously miserable person, with one leg, using crutches, absolutely harmless to anyone, being murdered with a shot to the chest at the top of a steep dead-end street, at night, under a torrential downpour. After a week of looking for a resolution that made sense, I needed to play around a bit with the ants. Especially after the only suspect confessed that he'd lied in our first interview, which brings us back to nothing."

Despite the difficult week, the weekend with Irene made Espinosa forget crimes, criminals, police stations, policemen, investigations, and trials, and everything else that connected him to a world he felt more distant from with each passing day.

Saturday was the day to take the kids to the club, but Camila asked a friend whose kids were the same age and who was also a member to take Cíntia and Fernando with her. They decided to have lunch together at the club's restaurant. That way she and Aldo would have the whole morning to talk without being interrupted.

The two previous nights, she hadn't managed to question her husband about the night of the dinner party, not because she hadn't tried but because he kept avoiding the subject. She didn't want their silences to become chronic. They had just finished breakfast; she waited for Aldo to glance at the headlines and asked: "Why don't we talk about the subject we've been avoiding?"

"There's not a lot to talk about."

"We can at least update the little we've already said. The night it all began, something must have happened at the end of that street, something you didn't tell me. We drove home without your saying a single word, and you remained silent until we went to bed. When the police called to see if you'd seen anything out of the ordinary, you thought you ought to tell me something, but you ended up saying nothing: that you hadn't told the cops anything because you hadn't seen anything. After a day or two, you confessed that you'd lied to the cops . . . not exactly lied, but had made up a story, since you didn't remember anything at all. . . . And from what I know of you, something must have happened yesterday or the day before yesterday. Am I right?"

"You are . . . as always."

"No, Aldo. Not as always. Or, if you want, it's the other way around: as always, I know almost nothing. If you want to tell me, I'm ready to listen to you, but if you don't want to say anything, then we can change the subject and go to the club."

"At the beginning I really didn't remember anything. Then I started getting some flashes of memory . . . until the chief showed me the photo."

"What photo?"

"Of the dead guy . . . except that he was alive. It was a trick. I was shocked, and then I suddenly remembered."

"Remembered what?"

"That when I went to get the car I saw a body on the pavement. I turned on the lights and went up closer . . . there was a bloodstain in the middle of his chest. The man only had one leg . . . he was dead. . . . I jumped into the car and picked you up so we could get out of there."

"Did you tell this to the policeman?"

"Not immediately . . . only after that Rogério Antunes, who'd also parked up there, told the officer that he'd seen a body on the ground."

"And why didn't he say anything before?"

"Out of fear."

"Of what?"

"Who knows . . . fear . . . fear of getting involved in a police investigation. Except that after he told the truth he called me to tell me what he'd done. And then I didn't have a choice but to tell the officer that I had been lying too."

"And what did he do?"

"What do you mean?"

"Did he believe you?"

"Who knows. . . . Why? You don't believe me?"

"The main thing is whether he, the officer in charge of the case, believes you."

"For me, the main thing is that you, my wife, believe me."

"If that was really important, you would have told me this before you told him. And I think that the only reason you told him and me was that you were forced to."

"That's unfair. . . . The way you're talking, I get the impression that you don't trust me."

"Don't trust you? What we're talking about here took place more than a week ago, nine days ago to be precise, and only now, after I pressure you, do you decide to tell me. Who's not trusting whom?"

"I was disturbed."

"You must have been, to get involved in a situation that would have been extremely simple if you and this other guy hadn't lied to the police."

"Now I've told him the truth."

"Put yourself in his place, Aldo. The man is a police chief, suspicion is his job, you've already told three different stories—why do you think he'll believe the latest one? Or why do you think he'll believe any of them?"

"There's nothing else besides that."

"Are you sure? You're not hiding anything from me?"

"I already said that my memory still has holes in it. I still don't remember everything that happened that night."

"The only time you saw that man was when he was dead on the ground?"

"Of course."

"For me there's no 'of course' about it, but if you think that's all, then we can go to the club. I suggest you improve your expression and your mood. Both are awful."

When he got off work on Monday, Espinosa agreed to meet with Welber and Ramiro, who wanted to have a chat. After the reforms that changed police stations into "legal" stations, the old totems—weapons—had been replaced by the new totem—the computer—before which all prostrated themselves, worshipping the new divinity: the Internet. Espinosa had never been very handy with totems and had always been profoundly indifferent to all kinds of divinities. When Ramiro and Welber entered his office, he was struggling with all his strength against everything that began with the letters "www."

"Need some help, Chief?"

"Afterward. First I want to know what you need."

"It's like this, Chief," Ramiro began. "You filed away, quote unquote, the case of the homeless man, which you said hadn't even become a case. We happen to know—the 'we' is Welber and I—that you're still investigating on your own, without any help, not even from the police Web site. We saw what a hard time you were having when we came into the room. What we want to do is offer our unofficial help, not working overtime, not getting anyone else involved, and not expecting anything in return. We know you, sir, and we know that you're not going to rest until you're done with this story, whatever it is. That's it. How can we help?"

"Something tells me the death wasn't an accident. One way to check it out is to search the Internet for any leads for a dark-skinned man in his fifties, missing a leg, thin, tall, homeless, known as Skinny, who lived in the Pavão-Pavãozinho slum and hung out in Copacabana and Ipanema. Unlikely that he had a criminal record. I think we have a case only if we can get any little detail about the man's story. The only thing we know is how he died. Let's try to re-create his past, including learning his real name. I suggest you visit the Forensic Institute and ask the fellow who performed the autopsy about how long ago he lost his leg. There must be a record of the surgery, of the doctor who performed it, and the patient. Depending on the cause of the amputation, there might even be a police record. The date will only be a rough estimate, which will make your work harder. In this initial phase of research, you can use part of the day, the morning or the afternoon, to consult the hospital archives. Start with the bigger, older ones."

The weekend had been the worst one possible, though it seemed normal on the surface. Aldo played with the kids, had lunch and talked with his friends, and kept his relationship with Camila within the boundaries of the normal day-to-day pattern. When he left for the office on Monday morning, he couldn't remember any of the conversations he'd had over the weekend. Not even those with Camila, with the exception of the discussion they'd had Saturday morning before they went to the club. He could remember what he'd done, but not what he'd said and heard.

As he always did when he was bothered by some personal problem, Aldo decided to walk to work—about twelve long blocks to the Avenida Atlântica—far enough to be able to think the problem over. But there was no thinking over, only distraction, breaking his attention into little circumstantial events; he even took an interest in passersby, as if he were a tourist walking through Ipanema for the first time, an interest he knew was fake, as if he were only playing the role of a curious newcomer, when in fact he wasn't interested in what he was seeing. The hurried rhythm of his steps belied his superficial interest in the reality around him. It was neither thought nor attention. His mind was simply scattered.

He dedicated the morning to helping the interns and discussing current projects with Mercedes. The discussions were exclusively technical, with no reference to personal issues. At the time when they usually went down for lunch, Aldo decided to remain in the office, since he wasn't hungry; he would get a sandwich later. Mercedes left with Henrique and Rafaela, headed toward the self-service place they visited when they were short of money. The afternoon was unusually silent. At the end of the day, as soon as the interns left, Mercedes came into the conference room, which was also Aldo's office. He was sitting with his chair facing the window, looking out at the late-afternoon landscape of Copacabana Beach.

"Seeing ghosts in the window?"

Aldo turned around, startled.

"Sorry if I scared you . . ."

"Mercedes . . . I thought everyone had gone."

"Henrique and Rafaela left. It's just us."

As she spoke, Mercedes pushed a wheeled chair up to Aldo. She stopped just short of him, the arms of the two chairs touching, which made their own arms touch lightly.

"Returning to the sentence that frightened you: the ghosts still won't leave you alone?"

"I still don't know if they're ghosts or real people. I also don't know which of those possibilities scares me more."

"You didn't talk to your wife about this? She can help you."

"She's my wife . . . she's not my therapist."

"Of course, that's not what I'm saying. . . . But she is someone who knows how to deal with these questions."

"It's not that simple. She's directly involved in my life, so it's no longer a subjective question; it's something that affects both of us equally."

"Then the best thing would be for you to talk to a third person, someone who's not directly involved, who can listen to you and help you. I've already offered my help. I'm not a professionally qualified listener, but I can offer you receptivity, interest, love."

"You're a love, Mercedes."

"Not yet . . . but I can become one."

The sun had already set, but it had not yet grown entirely dark, and the lights of the office hadn't been turned on. He could still make out all the objects in the room with reasonable clarity, as well as the contours of Mercedes, who placed her hand on Aldo's arm and moved her face toward his.

"You don't think it's time to chase away the monsters? You've been suffering for days and nothing has been done to lighten your burden."

"And what can we do, Mercedes?"

"We can start . . . by taking off our clothes."

PART II

Ever since he'd started at the new school, the boy had been given his parents' permission to go to school by himself. It was an extraordinary feeling of freedom, perhaps the greatest he'd ever felt. His new uniform clearly signaled to anyone who saw him that he was no longer in elementary school. A few days before classes began, his mother walked him along the most direct route, with the smallest number of street crossings, and pointed out all the more dangerous ones. Within the first week, he had already discovered that besides the route his mother had shown him, he could go from home to school down two very busy streets—the most direct path—or down residential side streets, or in a zigzag, using a combination of both. The choice depended on how much time he had to get to school, on the way there, or to get home, on the way back. The shortest route involved going down a street one block from his own street to one of the main streets of the neighborhood, and then walking four more blocks to the school. With a steady pace and no stops, it wouldn't take more than twenty minutes. If he took the other routes the time could double, not only because of the distance but also because of the little shops on those streets, which were more attractive to his eleven-year-old self than the big department stores on the two main avenues that cut across the neighborhood. The display of sweets in the window of the bakery exercised a fascination over him second only to the window of the little office-supply store on a side street, and both could demand so much attention that he would arrive home late. After the first few days, when the fright of freedom and the fear of the unknown were still greater than his desire to investigate, the boy slowly built up the courage to try out alternative routes and indulge in prolonged detours. The quadrilateral formed by the big parallel avenues and the four smaller cross streets offered a multitude of combinations as rich as they were mysterious. He often ran into classmates. Some days, he started the walk alone and arrived with a little group that had gathered along the way. It was nice, but he preferred to go by himself: he had more freedom to change the itinerary and preserve the mystery of his new discoveries.

It happened a month before the end of the semester. The boy had chosen one of the alternative routes and was walking alone. He had just turned the corner onto the street with the office-supply shop, thinking that he would still have time to go in and examine the boxes of colored pencils with different brands and countries of origin. On his previous visits, he hadn't even examined half of them, nor the different drawing pads and imported pens. He'd walked down the first block and was halfway down the second when he saw in the distance two figures walking toward him: two boys, both older than he was, the older one tall and skinny. He immediately felt uneasy and was gripped by an uncontrollable fear. He stopped short and stayed still for a few seconds, long enough to be sure. It was him. He'd grown and gotten even skinnier, but the face was the same, with a cold, almost evil toughness, undoubtedly the same face. He didn't even look at the other boy's companion, since he was hypnotized by the figure that had terrorized his nights and penetrated his dreams in the years following their first encounter. And, just like that first time the older boy had hit him, he was petrified, incapable of any reaction, even flight. The other hadn't yet given the slightest sign of recognizing him, perhaps because of the distance. When they got closer he would recognize him and the whole scene would repeat itself, he was sure.

Despite the bright day, it seemed like everything was blacking out and he felt dizzy. He looked up and saw the sign of the office-supply shop a few feet away. He managed to move his legs and drag his feet up to the door of the store. He went in and hid in the back, hoping that the owner, who knew him, wouldn't call his name. It hadn't occurred to him that the attacker didn't know his name. He'd certainly seen him come into the store; what the boy didn't know was whether he'd recognized him. In the store there was no escape, he was hopelessly corralled; not even the owner of the shop was powerful enough to contain the aggressive fury of the older boy.

The boy melted into a shelf at the back of the store; the books and notebooks it held had fallen and he kicked them under the counter, and during the seconds that followed his entire being was focused on waiting for the moment in which the other boy would come into the store and tear him away from there. Now that he'd seen him in his uniform, he would know where he went to school and could wait for him after class or even ambush him on the way there. He waited. Maybe the aggressor was waiting for him to come out. Seconds that felt like hours passed, until the owner of the shop, noting his immobility and his expression of horror, asked what was going on, if he was feeling bad, why he was so pale, and other questions that went unanswered in the boy's momentary deafness. He couldn't respond and he could hardly see the man who was asking him the questions. The only image present in his consciousness was that of the repeated blows to his face. The man asked again if he was feeling all right and if he wanted him to call his home. No, he didn't. The only thing he wanted was for the older kid to go away so he could leave the store. Besides, if they were walking in the opposite direction, it was because they were going to his house. He was less than two blocks from school, but he didn't know if he was already late, though that was the only place he could go now. He was sure of one thing: the other kid had not passed by the front of the store. Either he was waiting for him to leave or he had turned the corner at the end of the block.

The owner of the shop helped him gather up the books and notebooks underneath the counter and walked him to the door, still asking if he felt like going on by himself. No. He didn't. He wanted the protection of an adult. But he wouldn't say that to anyone, even if he was threatened with the same attack he had suffered as a child. At the door, with the shopkeeper beside him, he examined every inch of the street, inside the buildings, behind the parked cars, until he was sure the other wasn't there. At school he had diarrhea and fever. His mother came and took him home.

From that day on, he was absolutely sure that the situation would repeat itself throughout his life. He learned, a while later, through friends, that the boy's name was Nilson.

1

The night before, Aldo hadn't eaten at home and hadn't called to say he'd be late. He got in after eleven and found Camila in bed but still awake. It was clear to her that he would have rather found her asleep. She hadn't been lying there waiting for explanations or to preach to her husband. Besides, she was perfectly aware that ever since the night of the dinner on the Rua Mascarenhas de Moraes, the events of that night had morphed and taken on scary contours that threatened her husband's fragile emotional balance. The memory loss made it a terror for him: an absence that could, at any moment, become a presence, looming up out of his own mind. She understood all that, and she was ready to help him if necessary. What she didn't want was to have a marriage full of silences, evasive behavior, and lies.

She left home and headed to the gym a bit before nine. The shops were still not open, and most of the people on the streets of Ipanema were those arriving to open their businesses or waiting for transportation to take them downtown. The weather was still nice, and the luminosity of the morning announced a hot day, which didn't bother her, since the external temperature affected neither the gym nor her office. Aldo was still on her mind, and she couldn't decide what to do about his crisis.

Her afternoon patients brought no news, content to repeat their usual litany of woes. At the end of the day she opened the door to Antonia. Her progress was much slower than Maria's, though both had started their analysis at about the same time. Antonia tended to silences, which occasionally extended to the entire session. Like Maria, she didn't reject Camila's light physical contact, but she still hadn't reached the brazenness of her fellow patient. They were her two Marias. It wasn't strange that Maria of Ipanema was freer with her body than Maria of Portugal.

Antonia spent more than half of the session in silence. She broke it by saying:

"I didn't know that it was possible for something to happen like it did in the last session."

"What do you think is or isn't possible?"

"I don't know. But I didn't know I could."

"But you didn't say anything."

"I didn't know what to say. I thought you would go on . . . but you didn't."

"Is that what you wanted?"

"I think so."

"You think so or it is so?"

"It is."

"Still?"

"I think so . . ."

Camila left her office when it was getting dark. She liked the little walk, two blocks, to her house: the windows alight and the colored signs, the lights of the cars, the streetlamps. There were days in which she preferred that nocturnal landscape to the bright light of the early mornings. The steady tropical light tans the body but wearies the spirit, so much so that she sometimes longed for a week of grayness and rain. And she felt it was time for the weather to change. She didn't want to go home. She wanted to see her kids, but not her husband. It had happened before. Though the distance was short, she stretched it out as long as she could, lingering in front of the most interesting shops and entering the little malls to gaze in the windows. She had no desire to purchase anything: she needed to look, and to think. As usual when she felt this way, she didn't stay too long and soon headed home. She and Aldo usually got home around the same time, which wasn't the case that evening, just like the night before. She waited almost an hour before she got his call. He said he'd have to stay late at work . . . that she should go ahead and eat without him . . . that he'd eat something when he got home. He didn't have to say any of that. She'd already eaten and wasn't waiting for him. After staying with the kids until their bedtime, she went to her room, found a movie on TV, and sat waiting . . . not for her husband, but for herself: for herself to be ready to go to sleep. That happened before Aldo arrived.

Restarting the investigation, even if it was only semi-official, was a relief for Espinosa, who was disappointed by the interviews he'd conducted the week before. What was most disturbing wasn't how little he'd learned from his meetings with the people who could have had some relation to the scene of the crime but the near impossibility of imagining who those people were, what they thought, what they felt, what kind of relationship they had with the world around them. The friendlier they were, the more impenetrable. That was the case of Rogério Antunes, who spent his days at the Yacht Club: it was hard to know what he did for a living, if that made any difference. He probably didn't even have a boat. He was a member of the Yacht Club just as he could have been a member of the Racing Club. Boats or horses, it didn't make any difference: Espinosa himself didn't sail or ride. And there was the architect Aldo Bruno and his beautiful wife, Camila. They gave an impression of complete distance from the world, and from each other . . . as if they lived in closed worlds that were enough for them. They seemed like sad people, though they were young, good-looking, and rich, or maybe precisely for that reason: perhaps their abundance wore on them. At first he had tried to get to the homeless man through these people, and now he would try to get to them through the homeless man.

The results of the preliminary investigations conducted by Welber at the Forensic Institute and by Ramiro on the Internet were not promising. The man who'd performed the autopsy thought the amputation had taken place at least twenty years before. Which meant that the victim had been little more than thirty years old at the time of the surgery. Ramiro's check of the police archives produced hundreds of results for the keywords he typed in, but nothing that pointed to a single person—and that was just in the archives that had been computerized. Inspector Ramiro considered that a personal inquiry with his friends in the two precincts in Copacabana would turn up more. That was all they had accomplished thus far.

Aldo was convinced he had done something incredibly stupid—having been entrapped by the suggestion-seduction of Mercedes. True, she was a master. The right time, the right place, a pretty woman, an offer he couldn't refuse. But the fact was, she was a colleague in a workplace where, besides the two of them, only two twenty-year-old interns worked. Mercedes was twenty-five. The consequences of his behavior wouldn't be good for him, no matter how attractive she was. They wouldn't be good for Mercedes, and the inevitable repercussions they would have on his relationship with Camila wouldn't be good either. And they wouldn't be good for his firm. Mercedes now had power over him, personally and professionally. All because he hadn't been able to resist an invitation that wouldn't have had the same implications if it had happened with the same Mercedes in another place and at another point in his personal life. Camila had an incredible ability to pick up his personal and emotional conflicts; it wouldn't take long before she started asking questions. Besides, he'd felt weak, too emotionally fragile to resist Mercedes's stronger determination, which, after all, was designed to offer him her body and her affection to smooth over the momentary neediness he was going through. It was unfair to blame Mercedes for it. He was scared for no reason, at least no reason involving her. There was only one objective problem that he couldn't solve: it would be impossible for Henrique and Rafaela, the interns, not to notice what was going on between him and his assistant, and that wasn't good for his office. The fact is, though, that he was feeling better. Mercedes had given him the confidence to overcome the crisis caused by the policeman's insistence on knowing stupid details. But more than anything, there was her exuberant shamelessness, in contrast to Camila's near timidity in bed, which had left him looking forward to new encounters. His wife was more inquisitive than amorous. The doubt she'd subtly shown in their last conversation about Chief Espinosa was proof of that. She had even doubted what he'd told her about what had happened at the end of that street. It was understandable that the officer would be suspicious, that was expected; but for his own wife to doubt what he was saying during an intimate conversation was depressing.

As he'd been doing for the last two days, he walked to work while thinking over the changes in his relationship with Camila and the change in the nature of his relationship with Mercedes. In the case of Mercedes, if the change was dangerous, it was also a source of great pleasure.

It was after nine when he got to work. Henrique and Rafaela were there alone. Mercedes didn't come in all morning, and she didn't call, either. She arrived after lunch, visibly excited. She barely acknowledged the interns, went into Aldo's office, and spoke softly while watching the door:

"I found a place for us!"

"What?"

"I found a place for us . . . a place for us to stay."

"Place? What are you talking about?"

"Aldo, you don't want us to have to keep meeting in the office. . . . I mean, of course we'll still see each other here, but to work, not to screw! An old college friend, Luíza, is going to spend some time in Spain on a graduate fellowship and left me her apartment. The fellowship isn't for very long, but it'll give us time to find something else before she gets back. So the office stays the office, and our homes as well."

"What . . . where . . ."

"Don't worry about anything. Luíza is an architect and has very good taste, so she didn't want to rent it out and was happy to lend it to me, because that way I'll keep an eye on it. So at the end of the afternoon we can go there. She left last night. It's already ours . . . for three months."

The only person who knew the dead man's name, and anything they could use to learn more about him, was Joca, the former janitor at the Horizon Club, who had known Skinny when they both lived in the Pavão-Pavãozinho slum. But Joca, or whatever his name was, had disappeared off the face of the earth. The informers connected to the community in Pavão-Pavãozinho knew several Jocas, but none corresponded to the limited description of the ex-employee of the club. The most they got from the street dwellers of Copacabana was that the man known as Skinny or One-Leg was a loner. Espinosa thought it was incredible that someone could have lived all of his apparent fifty years in Copacabana without leaving a single trace, a single mark, without any connection, positive or negative, to any-one. Skinny, or One-Leg, was a ghost. The only thing that gave him an identity was the lack of a leg.

Without any facts to go on, Espinosa sketched an imagi-nary story for the homeless man, though he thought the real story couldn't be too far off. Skinny would have been born in the early fifties in one of the Copacabana slums, maybe the old slum of Cantagalo, son of a single mother and an unknown father. He probably lost touch with his mother before he was ten, and grew up in a group of home-less kids, without the slightest education or maternal care. He survived thanks to alms and petty thefts until he reached adulthood. When he was around thirty, he'd had a leg amputated (because of an accident or the gangrene result-ing from a wound). From thirty to fifty, the only major change in his life had come from the difficulties related to missing a leg and the use of crutches. He was shot to death while doing what he'd always done: asking for food.

Espinosa thought this mini-biography could be printed up, leaving a blank space for the name, to serve as a pattern for the population of unfortunates who survived in the city. The missing leg was just a detail.

Welber had chosen the Hospital Miguel Couto, the biggest hospital in the Zona Sul of Rio, as the place where the homeless man would have had his leg removed. In fact, the operation could have been performed in any hospital, but Miguel Couto was the most likely. They had thousands of files organized in chronological order. Even if he found a matching reference—patient so-and-so, male, thirty years old, dark-skinned, etc., amputation of the right leg— nothing would guarantee that so-and-so was Skinny. In the hope of finding promising entries, he had noted the names of the possible candidates he'd found in the police files in case he came across them in the hospital files. Having done that, Welber could figure out where Skinny had hung out, what he'd done, who he'd spent time with, and who he hadn't gotten along with. It wasn't the easiest of jobs.

Over the course of the week, Aldo went home only to shower and sleep. He got home as late as possible and left before Camila awoke. Once or twice, he spoke to the kids before they went to school; he'd barely spoken at all to Camila since the weekend, when they'd discussed what was going on with him. It wasn't the first time Aldo had been overcome by a kind of silent panic accompanied by flight from a dangerous situation. Camila thought the dangerous situation wasn't necessarily real, or not totally real. In her opinion, which she'd already shared with her husband, the episode involving the murder worked as a trigger for a state of panic whose real cause was something else that he himself didn't realize, or was hiding. It was Thursday and had been almost a week since Aldo had started hiding from her.

Her patients Maria and Antonia were what reality offered her as a reward in her parallel clinical world: daring and pleasure, indispensable ingredients for what she called the cocktail of life. She had managed to get them scheduled for alternate days. Seeing them both on the same day would force her to risk diminishing the intensity she required. Antonia was the big surprise—which in no way overshadowed the charms of Maria—and Camila suspected that she had surprised her even more over the course of the treatment. Antonia and her sweet, though almost completely lost Portuguese accent. It was difficult to imagine a more perfect harmony between the beauty of her body and the beauty of her voice. Even when she said nothing and lay motionless, there was sweetness and suppleness there. Maria was devilish, but Antonia was divinely perverse.

Ever since he'd met Camila Bruno, Espinosa had considered her the stronger partner in the marriage. Aldo was anxious and evasive, while Camila was vigorous and direct, and was in charge of her own life.

A society columnist who owed Espinosa a favor gave him a brief history of the Brunos and of Rogério Antunes. Before he'd married Camila, whose maiden name was Moreira da Rocha, Aldo had worked for twelve years at an engineering firm that produced cookie-cutter apartment buildings for the upper middle class. As business fell off, Aldo was replaced by an intern. After working for a few construction firms, he abandoned architecture and, together with two colleagues, opened a fancy paper store, which sold imported materials to architects, designers, painters, and writers. They were forced to close after six months. After that, when the cell phone rage began, he opened a franchise in a shopping center, but it lasted only a couple of months longer than his previous venture. He tried to go back into architecture, but the market was even worse than when he'd lost his first job. That was when he met Camila and his life was radically transformed, the columnist confided, thanks to the aristocratic name and the immense fortune of the Moreira da Rocha family.

As for Rogério Antunes, he had been born rich and got richer with each passing day, without ever having to do anything to increase that fortune, though he had done much to try, unsuccessfully, to diminish it. Risking a comparative diagnosis of the two, the columnist said that Rogério Antunes and Aldo Bruno could be considered opposite sides of a single psychological profile: while one was an inconsequential manic, for whom the world was one endless party, the second was a chronic depressive. And with that wife, the columnist added. Espinosa avoided asking if the final comment was aesthetic or ethical.

In his interview with her in her office, the doctor hadn't seemed the slightest bit intimidated or defensive. To the contrary: on a few occasions she had even confronted him fearlessly. She was definitely an imposing feline, beautiful, sensual, powerful. Compared to her, the husband seemed like a domestic cat.

He managed to arrange another meeting with Dr. Camila for that very day, at six P.M., one week after the first. Espinosa inferred that this was after her last appointment, so they could converse freely.

As he'd done the first time, Espinosa arrived a half hour early and went into the same bookstore to check out the new arrivals. At six on the dot, carrying a small plastic bag, he rang the doorbell of Camila's office. There was no sign indicating that it was a place of business.

"Chief Espinosa," Camila said, looking at the bag, "I don't know if you've come for me or for the bookstore."

"Certainly for you, Doctor; the bookstore is just an excuse."

"Anything new?"

"At the bookstore or at the precinct?"

"The bookstore, of course."

"A new and excellent translation of Faulkner."

"You surprise me, sir."

"I hope it's a pleasant surprise."

"Of course. Certainly. And at the precinct, anything new?"

"Unfortunately not. Two weeks have gone by and there's been no progress. That's why I've come back here."

"And you've come looking for me in connection with my husband."

"Not only. I think that everyone involved in the events

of that night is hiding something. Hiding something important about the death of the homeless man."

"Did the homeless man have a name?"

"He was known by the nickname Skinny . . . which isn't a name, it's an adjective. All we have are adjectives, when what we need are nouns. The only thing we have is a body at the Forensic Institute."

"Among the people who you suspect are hiding something is my husband, you think."

"That's what I think."

"And you're asking me to reveal what my husband might be hiding?"

"Roughly put, yes."

"Officer, the subjectivity of every person is his most inaccessible part, for others and for himself. The fact that I am married to him does not mean I have access. I would even say that because we are more intimate the defenses are even stronger."

"You are right. But because of this intimacy, you might have noticed mood swings that might indicate certain external changes of uncommon intensity."

"Perhaps. He is my husband."

"Dr. Camila, I'm not asking you to incriminate your husband, I'm asking you to clear up certain ambiguities."

"In order to do that, Officer, I'd have to unravel Aldo's entire life. He doesn't talk much, and he has more than his share of worries. . . . So I'm not going to put myself in the impossible position of becoming my own husband's therapist."

"Was he always like that?"

"How?"

"Worried."

"I've only known him for eleven years, so I can't say what he was like before that."

"But he must have said something about his childhood."

"The only thing he said was that his childhood was turbulent."

While he was waiting for the elevator, Espinosa wondered why Dr. Camila had been out of breath when she'd opened the door for him. . . . But that question wasn't very pertinent to his investigation, though there was another detail that invited interesting speculations: the doctor's shirt had been on inside out.

It was early evening when he went out onto the street and decided to walk a bit through Ipanema at dusk. He was more interested in the movement on the sidewalks, the people carrying their grocery bags, and the shop windows than in the predictable sunset on Ipanema Beach, which dazzled locals as well as tourists. He was much more perturbed by Dr. Camila than by the monotonous repetition of the sun setting over the Atlantic.

Aldo let Thursday go by, and only on Friday did he go inspect the apartment Mercedes had arranged as a short-term solution for their trysts. She had referred to the "short term," obviously indicating that there would be a "long term" once the three months were up. The building, on a side street in Copacabana, was only five blocks from the office, a typical 1950s building with four apartments on each of eight floors, entirely residential. Mercedes was excited about it. They walked hurriedly, holding hands, toward the address she had noted on a piece of paper, which she had then placed in his wallet so he couldn't forget. The fact that they were holding hands in the middle of the Avenida Atlântica and then on the Rua Bolívar, when lots of people were around, could be credited to Mercedes's excitement, or to her deliberate intention to make their intimate relationship known. He had to be careful with these supposed oversights if he wanted to stay married, though he couldn't hide his pride at being seen holding hands with Mercedes. They left the office before lunch, which would give them at least two hours to inaugurate what she was calling "our *garçonnière*." Mercedes was young, impetuous, passionate, and he thought that the three months would be long enough to tamp down her expectations of something long-term. The apartment was small but pleasant, though there was no time, that first day, for detailed observations. Mercedes was anxious to use the encounter to prove her excellence as a lover and a companion—which indisputably helped Aldo feel better, though it also frightened him.

They got back to the office at a quarter to three. The rest of the afternoon was interrupted by meetings during which Mercedes's begging eyes sought to meet Aldo's passionate gaze, or even some subtle gesture indicating that something had changed in their relationship. Nothing changed until nightfall, when, after the interns had left, Aldo had to tell her that at work or in public there could be no signs of affection between them.

"So we can fuck, but we can't show any affection?"

"We didn't fuck on the sidewalks, the streets, and the public parks, but in bed, inside a room, in an apartment with a locked door. The question isn't what we do or don't do, but what we can do in public."

"Because you're married?"

"Of course."

"And what am I? A whore? I can get you in trouble, but you can't get me in trouble?"

"Mercedes, you knew I was married."

"I did. But so did you. See you tomorrow."

It was seven in the evening when Espinosa picked up Irene at her apartment building and they walked through Ipanema in the direction of Leblon. The good taste Irene employed in her graphic design was also reflected in her dress, her walk, her gestures, a good taste that in no way could be confused with affectation or refinement. Slim, almost as tall as Espinosa, she walked with the lightness of a ballerina. It was five blocks from her building to the canal of the Jardim de Alá, which separated the neighborhoods of Ipanema and Leblon. The breeze coming from the sea softened the summer heat and made Espinosa's walk to the end of Ipanema more pleasant. He was going in search of a little restaurant he had noticed during one of his visits to Dr. Camila. And he liked the feel of the end of the evening and the beginning of the night in Ipanema, so different from the more frenetic rhythm of Copacabana.

"We're not going to your apartment?" Irene asked.

"First we're going to have a glass of wine."

"Somewhere special?"

"Recently I've been coming over here to visit a therapist and paying visits to the bookstore that's nearby. I came across a little restaurant that looks extremely pleasant and charming. It's not far. It's on the last block of Ipanema."

"You've been seeing a therapist?"

"Not exactly. Visiting a therapist."

"And might I know why you've been visiting a therapist?"

"Because of her husband."

"Is there something going on between you and the husband, dear?"

"More or less. Not an affair, a murder case."

"It's almost the same thing."

While they talked about the case and examined the elegant stores in the neighborhood, they walked the five blocks. The restaurant was really a little shop selling wines and cold cuts, with four or five tables for steady customers. They took the only available table, chose a wine, and ordered a cheese plate.

"Now tell me, what's the story with this therapist?"

"She's the wife of the architect who did the house up on the Rua Mascarenhas de Moraes. Both were at the dinner party. The guy is skittish, psychologically complicated, and

I'm trying to find a window to get in there, since the doors are closed—to get inside his head. Since I'm a cop and not a psychiatrist or psychoanalyst, I'm not subtle or theoretically equipped enough to get directly to the suspect. So I'm trying to get there through his wife, who, besides being his wife, is also a shrink."

"And she must be pretty."

"That's just a detail."

"You're avoiding the question."

"Yes. She's pretty."

"Of course, since otherwise you wouldn't have gone to see her three or four times."

"Twice."

"And?"

"Nothing. She won't help someone who's suspicious of her husband."

"Which she's right about."

"I know. I said the same thing to her. I'm not asking her to turn in her husband, I'm just asking her to tell me about the kind of person he is. She said he was nervous, that his childhood was difficult. . . . That's what I want her to talk about."

"And she doesn't want to."

"She doesn't quite trust my story, that I'm interested in her husband's childhood, in his worries."

"Of course. She knows what you'd take away from that."

"She might know, but I don't. I'm just prodding around here, like I'd be prodding around a hole in the ground. . . . You never know, something might turn up."

"And the story about his worries. . . . Who doesn't have them?"

"It's true. . . . Except some worried people's worries are more worrying than others."

"I think I heard that somewhere else."

"Maybe. The fact is, the only two people who were definitely at the scene of the crime were two people invited to the dinner party, and both of them have already fed me opposite versions of the simple act of going to get a parked car. Nobody went up that street—there's a guard there, day and night—and nobody came out of the building at the end of the street. It's almost impossible for someone to have come out of the woods at the top of the hill; it's high and hard to get there. . . . That's a lot of effort to put into killing a man who was already half dead anyway."

"Espinosa, this place is great, but I feel like we've got more to talk about. Let's get another bottle and some snacks and take a taxi back to the Peixoto District. What do you think?"

"Great idea. I still want to talk to you about fiction."

"What fiction?"

"Fiction . . . literary or otherwise. About pretending."

"What does that have to do with the case?"

"Everything."

It was hard for Aldo to go home on Friday night. He hadn't used the car or any other means of transportation to go from home to work. But it wasn't the walk, nearly three kilometers, that made it hard: it was the weekend with Camila and the kids, the club on Saturday afternoon, the family conversations. He didn't dislike his wife and kids; to the contrary—he liked them a lot and would do anything for them. But during the last two weeks he'd found that he couldn't stand to be around them. That was why he walked so slowly, stopping along the way whenever anything caught his eye. Even so, he eventually arrived back home. Late enough for the kids to have already eaten. Camila was waiting for him. The table wasn't set and there was no movement in the kitchen to indicate an impending meal. Camila noted her husband's surprise and said:

"In case you've forgotten, we agreed to eat out tonight."

"We and who else?"

"Nobody, dear, we're not pleasant to be around. It's better for us to go out alone . . . though in each other's company."

"Don't be ironic, Camila."

"I'm not. I don't like irony. I'm just saying what I think about the two of us, as a couple, right now. I'm not being judgmental, I'm just saying what we're like."

They chose a restaurant close to home, not so much because the food was so good but because it wasn't loud: they could talk without having to shout. Not that either of them expected a very animated conversation. In any case, the conversation started off with an almost bureaucratic question from Aldo.

"So, how was your day?"

"Regular . . . except at the end of the day, when Chief Espinosa stopped by."

Aldo immediately raised his hand to his cheek. He sat looking at Camila, waiting for her to continue.

"Honey, why don't you have a little bit of wine to relax. The chief is not the devil incarnate. Apparently he's as confused as I am about the death of the beggar."

Aldo slurped down the wine as if it were beer.

"What did he want?"

"He wanted to know what you were like."

"What?"

"That's right. He didn't want to know what you had done that night, or where you were on a certain afternoon. He wanted to know if you were a person who was psychologically unusual . . . what your childhood was like . . . things like that. Of course I didn't say anything."

"What's his deal? Does he think he's a shrink?"

"Some people think it's enough to ask about someone's childhood and sex life to get to the bottom of things. But I don't think that's what he's trying to do. Despite his pleasant voice and his distracted appearance, he's not stupid or naïve. He's trying to reverse the normal police procedures. He wants to know who, out of the people who were at the scene of the crime, might have the psychological predisposition to shoot someone. He's no longer interested in knowing who had a gun or who saw the beggar first; he wants to know who, under high pressure and upset by powerful forces, could have shot a stranger in the middle of the night in a thunderstorm."

"In those conditions, anyone who was armed could be liable to shoot."

"Then it's lucky you weren't armed. . . . You could have done it."

Camila's phrase dissipated a bit of the shadow that had fallen on the dinner since she'd mentioned Espinosa. Camila knew, from experience, that her husband couldn't talk about another potentially threatening topic. He could talk about a single thing until he considered the subject exhausted, but he couldn't then move to a second or third topic of similar intensity. During the rest of the dinner, they talked about friends, travel plans, and the weekend.

Irene had breakfast with Espinosa before leaving at around ten, saying she had to go to São Paulo that afternoon. He had long since learned not to ask about her sudden departures, since she would say that there was nothing sudden about them, that for instance, she had been planning that trip since the beginning of the week but just hadn't mentioned it to him. She, on the other hand, didn't ask what he was up to when he vanished for days on end without telling her why.

The fact is, he was there, on a Saturday morning that still hadn't decided whether it would be sunny or cloudy, having said good-bye to Irene and returned to the table for another cup of coffee and to decide what part of the house he would take care of first. There was the bookshelf, a permanent source of worry for his maid—and for him, ever since he had decided, years before, to erect a bookshelf made out of books. Of course, it wasn't destined exclusively to contain books, it was simply *made out of* books. He called it a "shelf in its purest state," which meant a line of books on the ground in the living room, and then atop those books another level of books lying flat, and then more on top of those. The shelf was already as tall as the doorway, creating a compact mass of books three meters tall and two meters wide, six square meters of shelving without a single screw or piece of wood. It was a magnificent piece of engineering, one he planned to keep exactly as it was, putting off as long as possible its eventual collapse. The other problem was the toaster that toasted only one side of the bread, which made breakfast a bit more work. A while back, he'd bought a new toaster, but he hadn't gotten used to it. For days, he'd kept them side by side, using the old one, until he finally put away the new one. And there was the problem of the floor: there were at least ten loose tiles, most of them in the living room. Those were the most consistent subjects of his Saturday morning reflections.

That morning, he decided to deal with the books, maybe because he didn't have anything else to do besides conducting a rigorous inspection of the structure, prodding a few of the books to see if it would fall over. . . . Since nothing fell over that morning, Espinosa could peacefully begin to read the paper, supposing that the next day he could take up the subject of the toaster or the loose tiles. The next day, Sunday, not that day, Saturday. But he thought of Sunday as a fiction in bad taste. All he could do was wait for the next Saturday. Until then he would try to rethink the current Saturday, with Irene absent. There were a few good options for a solitary weekend like the one just beginning. One was reading. On the coffee table and on the tables beside the sofa, a few books waited for his decision, whether they would be promoted to the table beside his lamp and reading chair. The latest acquisition was the Faulkner he had bought on his last visit to Dr. Camila. Espinosa chose two, both books he was rereading: the two linked stories of *The Wild Palms* and the extraordinary story of Kees Popinga by Simenon, which he'd read when he was twenty. He wanted to see how they would read twenty years on. He placed the two on the table beside his rocking chair.

The week began with a new stage in Ramiro and Welber's searches through the archives of the hospitals in the southern part of the city, and through their colleagues. With the material they obtained, they began to piece together hundreds of isolated, apparently unrelated facts, to see if they could determine the identity of the homeless man. Both dedicated Monday and Tuesday to this new stage of the search.

On Wednesday morning, Espinosa was informed by telephone of the death of Camila Bruno.

Camila Bruno was found dead in her office, stretched out on the sofa, entirely naked. The forensic expert who examined the scene suggested that she had been suffocated, but he couldn't find any signs of a struggle or any mark on her neck or nostrils. The only indication of possible suffocation were a few, almost invisible, hemorrhagic points on her eyes. Beside the sofa was a pillow, the probable murder weapon. Everything suggested murder, unless it was possible for someone to have committed suicide by forcing their own head into a pillow. At that point in the story, Espinosa interrupted his interlocutor, Chief Lajedo of the Fourteenth Precinct, who was telling Espinosa the story over the phone.

"Good night, Cinderella," said Espinosa.

"What?" said Lajedo.

"Sorry, I mean that the murderer must have sedated the victim with Rohypnol or something as powerful. Once she was asleep, all he had to do was press a pillow onto her face. Death without struggle or noise."

"It's possible," the other said, as if he had already reached the same conclusion.

"Lajedo, would you mind if I follow the case with you? I think it's related to a case I've been working on. I'd like to stop by your station and talk face-to-face."

"Sure, Espinosa, you're always welcome. That's why I'm calling: I saw in her agenda that you had come by twice in the last two weeks."

"I was talking to her about an investigation. That's what I want to discuss with you. Can we meet?"

"Of course. Before or after lunch?"

"Up to you."

"We've got plenty of time before lunch. Do you want me to come over or do you want to come over here?"

"I'll be there in fifteen or twenty minutes."

Espinosa told Welber and Ramiro the news of Camila's death along with the few details Lajedo had provided. He hoped to be back in time for lunch with them.

As soon as he got to the Leblon precinct and showed his badge, he was taken up to see the chief. They'd known each other since law school, when they had been classmates. Lajedo was experienced, Espinosa's age, and incorruptible and had something else in common with Espinosa: they both liked bookstores. He was less formal than Espinosa, in his clothing as well as in his general behavior, but he was friendly and warm—in personal relationships; professionally, he was strict and not necessarily friendly.

Lajedo welcomed Espinosa with open arms.

"Espinosa, an honor to have you among us."

"Great to see you, Lajedo. How's your family?"

"Still the same size, luckily. And yours?"

"A husband has come along."

"What do you mean?"

"My ex-wife remarried. They live in Washington, D.C."

The new generation of police stations were designed to all look alike, so that the only difference between Lajedo's and Espinosa's were the occupants. Lajedo asked not to be disturbed and the two went into his office, which was identical to Espinosa's.

Before asking his questions, Espinosa summed up the case of the homeless man's murder, including quick sketches of the people directly linked to it—Aldo and Camila Bruno. He also explained why he had seen Camila twice and the difficulty he was having in figuring out Aldo Bruno's story.

"Seems it will get even harder now," he concluded.

"It's possible. He could use his wife's death to close himself off even more."

"Who found the body?" Espinosa asked.

"He did."

"The husband?"

"Right. When she didn't come home for dinner, he called the office and her cell phone. Since she didn't pick up, he decided to go to the office, which is only two blocks away, to see what was going on. He asked the doorman, who said he hadn't seen her come out. Aldo went up and rang the bell. No answer. He found the door unlocked, went in, and saw his wife stretched out on the sofa . . . naked. He realized instantly that she was dead."

"Was someone with him when he saw that the door was unlocked?"

"No. He was alone."

"He said he saw instantly that she was dead?"

"He said it was obvious, though he didn't say how."

"Did he make any reference to her being naked?"

"Just that he didn't understand why."

"Did the preliminary examinations turn anything up?"

"There's no trace of sperm in her vaginal canal or in her anus, and there is no sign of sexual violence."

"No sign of sexual activity and no sign of violence or struggle. The nudity is what's hard to make sense of. Were her clothes on the floor or hanging somewhere?"

"They were sitting neatly on a chair."

"Any sign of cups, alcoholic beverages, drugs?"

"No. I agree with your hunch that she was drugged and then suffocated. As soon as the toxicological exam comes back I'll let you know."

"The drug could have been mixed with something she took from someone she knew, who took the cup when they left."

"Whoever did this didn't want to use physical force. She wasn't hit or anything like that—she was killed while she was asleep, without putting up a fight."

"I'd like to know if she took her own clothes off or if she was stripped after she took the drug or even after she was killed. Where did they find her agenda?"

"On top of the desk, in plain sight."

"Nobody saw anything? Nobody ringing the bell, rushing out . . ."

"She died between six and seven in the evening, the busiest time in the building, which has around a hundred commercial units."

"Fingerprints?"

"Many."

"Including mine, probably."

Before they wrapped things up, Lajedo passed Espinosa a hardcover notebook.

"I think you'll want to look at her agenda. There's a little room here where you can take your time without being disturbed. Later, if you think you need it, I can have it copied and sent over to you."

Espinosa spent almost an hour carefully reading the agenda and making notes in a little notebook. When he was through, he went back to the chief's office to thank him and place his own team at his disposal.

"Lajedo, our investigations are going to cross paths at some point. We might decide that they're not two different cases but part of a single story. Let's be sure to cooperate. I'll leave you the names and phone numbers of two of my colleagues. They're people I trust entirely: Inspector Ramiro and Detective Welber. Here they are," said Espinosa, passing a card to Lajedo. "As for me, you can call me whenever and wherever you need to."

"Thanks, Espinosa. I saw you came in a cab. Do you want me to send one of my men to take you back in a car?"

"Thanks, I'll take the bus. That will give me time to think."

There wasn't much to think about. He was sad about Camila Bruno's death. A smart, pretty, young woman . . . dead. Murdered. Why, and by whom? From Lajedo's description, it sounded like Camila had been stretched out on the sofa, like one of Goya's Mayas. No sign of struggle, violence, sexual aggression; there wasn't even a sign of sexual relations. Her agenda showed the names of the four patients she'd seen that afternoon: one man and three women. The same names figured in the book every week, and in the last week of the month their payments were noted. Some paid regularly with checks, some only in cash, which also was noted beside the amount. The patients were indicated only by their first names and, occasionally, phone numbers. There were no addresses. In the last two weeks, she had noted the day and time of the interviews he, Espinosa, had had with her. On the first it said "Chief Espinosa," followed by, in parentheses, the words "12th Precinct, Copacabana." On the second it just said "Chief Espinosa." No commentary, no additional notes. The first thing to do was to get in touch with Dr. Camila's patients and with Aldo Bruno. Espinosa didn't believe in coincidences. Two murders in two weeks, and in both cases Aldo Bruno was the first one on the scene. Could this be one of those rare cases in which the coincidence was simply a coincidence? There was also the possibility that Camila hadn't been nude when she was killed. Her nudity could then be a way of putting the police on the wrong track.

Espinosa waited until the next day to seek out Aldo Bruno. During their first telephone conversation, Aldo tried to get out of a meeting by saying he had already spoken to Lajedo and had nothing further to add. Espinosa pushed, saying that he could always appear at the station with his lawyer if that was more comfortable for him, but that it would be an unnecessary expense—he preferred to meet informally somewhere outside the station.

"Chief Espinosa, I haven't even buried my wife and you are summoning me to the station?"

"I'm not summoning you, I'm inviting you, and though I understand what you're going through, you can't forget that your wife was murdered. I'll call back tomorrow to arrange a meeting."

Camila's father made sure the body was released from the Forensic Institute as soon as possible. The funeral announcement took up ample space in the main newspapers, with her father, Armando Moreira da Rocha, reporting the death of his daughter Camila and inviting friends to the funeral that same afternoon. The name Bruno appeared nowhere in the announcement.

Espinosa hadn't seen Aldo Bruno since Camila's death. He didn't expect to speak to him immediately after the funeral, and he still didn't know what Aldo's relationship with Camila's family and friends was like. Though it was difficult to get to the chapel where the body was lying, he arrived there well in advance of the funeral. Aldo was inside, next to the body, but not on the same side of the coffin as her parents. It looked like a divided funeral: on the left side of the chapel were her parents and relatives; and on the other, Aldo, their children, and the couple's friends. Also with Aldo were Mercedes, the pretty architect, and the two interns from his office, Henrique and

Rafaela. Outside the chapel a soft rain was falling; instead of refreshing the air, it made the chapel even more hot and stuffy. People kept arriving, and nobody seemed to leave. At five o'clock on the dot the coffin was closed for its trip to the family resting place. Hundreds of open umbrellas covered the procession. There was already a little crowd around the tomb. There, the crowd was divided as well: parents and relatives on one side, Aldo, children, and friends on the other. Aldo was visibly devastated, standing next to his sad and perplexed kids, and the group of friends who still hadn't been able to make sense of what had happened. Espinosa watched the scene closely, without knowing for sure what he was looking for. He was interested in the faces and the gestures, since he had no way of hearing what people were saying. The circumstances compelled people to speak in low voices, though most remained silent. One thing was clear: Armando Moreira da Rocha looked at Aldo Bruno not with friendship or sympathy but with hatred. Aldo, on his side, stood staring off into the distance, opaquely, without sadness or emotion, as if suddenly nothing at all mattered. Once the ceremony was over, the crowd dispersed. Then those who'd stayed behind to speak to Camila's parents or Aldo left, and Aldo got up with the children, without so much as a glance at the Moreira da Rochas.

Aldo Bruno spent the weekend away from home and away from the office, not telling anyone where he was, not even his sister-in-law, who was watching the children.

Espinosa thought about calling some of the hotels where he could be staying, but he thought better of it before picking up the phone. He didn't think Aldo would be gone for long, since he was certainly gathering strength for what was about to hit him, especially the hatred of his father-in-law.

Armando Moreira da Rocha's power could be seen in the absolute lack of news about Camila's death in the papers. Few people knew that she had been murdered, and everything indicated that it would stay that way.

Espinosa felt paralyzed. The week had flown by and there he was, on Saturday morning, without Irene and without the urge to tackle any of the domestic projects that he had listed but not begun the week before. He hadn't managed to do any of the little jobs he needed to do, or even to read the Saturday paper, which he usually savored. He didn't feel like thinking about the two cases that had occupied him for the last few days. He tried to imagine what Aldo Bruno was doing at that moment. From what he knew of him, they had grown up in the same city, probably both in Copacabana, where the whole story had begun. It was very possible that they had even attended the same school at some point, and they had certainly passed each other in the street, in line at the movies, at a restaurant, in a bus. He was sure that at no point in the more than forty years he had lived had he noticed Aldo. And suddenly, somewhere between forty and fifty, Aldo had stepped out of the shadows and entered his life on two different occasions, in such dramatic ways. Aldo might not have been guilty of anything that had happened from the time he parked his car at the end of Mascarenhas de Moraes until the death of his wife four days before, but it was pretty intriguing that he had been the one to happen on both of those bodies. Espinosa knew instances of people being at the wrong place at the wrong time several times in a row, even though they had nothing to do with the events, though there was always some doubt about their innocence. And now nobody knew where Aldo Bruno was. The fact itself was not extraordinary; he had been gone for only twenty-four hours, which didn't even make it a disappearance. What caught his attention was the fact that Aldo had vanished so soon after his wife had been killed in such mysterious circumstances.

He went back to the paper. He scanned the headlines, removed the literary supplement, glanced at the bestseller lists, and dropped the rest of the paper on the ground without even looking at the crime page or the international news. He remained seated in his rocking chair, staring at the movement of the sunbeam that was slowly making its way across the room and that, according to his calculations, would reach his foot in fifteen minutes, at most—which was a good reason to stay seated: to see how close his calculation was. He stared at the sunlight. He thought that at that very moment the sun was illuminating half of the planet, arithmetically touching half the population of the world, something like three billion people, and he was the only one of them—more than that, the only *being*— who was being touched by that specific sunbeam . . . it was all his own . . . and not only then, but forever. And then he thought that if that was the best thing he could think about in that peaceful moment, that was a clear sign that humanity really hadn't worked out. He got up and went to wash the dishes from breakfast.

Monday morning. After stopping by the station to talk with his team about their current cases, Espinosa told Welber to speak to Camila's patients and put together a short profile of all of them, including their names, addresses, phone numbers, and professions.

"If I'm not mistaken, there are about ten of them. Also check out the ones who were released from therapy or who quit this year."

"Should I still keep working on the amputations?"

"Ask some of the new detectives if any of them can substitute for you while you seek out the patients. Call my cell phone if you find anything."

Espinosa rang the bell of Aldo Bruno's office without any warning, telling the doorman not to announce that he was coming up. The door was opened by one of the young interns. Almost at the same time, he heard Mercedes's voice, and she appeared in the room.

"Who is it, Rafaela?"

"It's that . . ."

"Good morning, Mercedes."

"Good morning, Officer."

"May I speak with Aldo?"

"He's not feeling well . . . he's still in shock."

"I understand. It's only natural."

"So . . ."

"But we can't wait any longer. I gave him the weekend; now I need to speak to him."

"May I come along? He's emotionally fragile."

"Don't worry, madam. I'm not the bad guy here. I'm not going to do anything to make it worse."

Mercedes let him in and led him to the door of Aldo's office. She knocked twice before opening it and, still clasping the handle, with the door slightly ajar, announced:

"Aldo . . . it's Chief Espinosa."

The architect, seated at his desk, looked up at her and then at the officer. He nodded his assent.

When Espinosa entered, she tried once again.

"May I?"

"I'm sorry, madam, it's a private conversation," he said, waiting for her to close the door.

Aldo Bruno had obviously not been working. The pencil in his hand pointed at a series of drawings, some geometric, some showing people, surrounded by various doodles.

"Good morning, Mr. Bruno. I tried to express my condolences on the day of the funeral, but I couldn't get near you. I'm terribly sorry about what happened. I saw your wife twice and I liked her very much."

"Thank you, sir. That's exactly what bothers and torments me. She really was an exceptional person. Young, pretty, smart, happy, nice. . . . So why? Why this . . . this . . . craziness . . . this cold, inhuman violence?"

"Maybe precisely because she was young, pretty, smart, nice . . ."

"That doesn't make sense to me. Nobody kills someone for that."

"I'm sorry, sir, but people kill one another for all kinds of reasons—and even for no reason at all."

"What do you want from me?"

"The way she died has already been partially explained. She was doped with a powerful sleeping medication and then suffocated with the pillow found on the floor beside her, next to the sofa. Death in those circumstances is pain-less. She didn't struggle, and her facial expression was calm. For me, what remains to be explained is why she was undressed. There was no sexual encounter, she had no marks, bruises, or scratches; so nothing indicates sexual violence. Why, then, was she naked?"

"I haven't been able to think of anything else since I found her."

"It's common enough for patients to fall in love with their therapists—she didn't mention anything like that to you?"

"No. She rarely said anything about her patients, and when she did it was only nice or funny things."

"When you got there you found the door was open?"

"Her door had to be locked from outside and inside. Who-ever killed her left and closed the door without locking it."

"When did you get to the office?"

"It was nine . . . give or take five minutes."

"Did you touch anything?"

"Only her. She was cold and obviously lifeless."

"You didn't take anything on your way out?"

"No. I wasn't thinking. When I saw she was dead, I left, closed the door, and stood outside . . . crying. Only when I stopped crying did I think to call someone."

"Do you know any of her patients?"

"No. I never saw a single one of them. I never went to her office once it was ready and she started seeing patients."

"You didn't ever stop by to pick her up when you were on your way home?"

"No. The office is so close to the house that she always liked to walk."

"A delicate question, Mr. Bruno: Were you going through what is sometimes called a difficult spot in your marriage?"

"No. We always got along perfectly. Of course, in ten years of marriage there is the occasional issue, but nothing that ever lasted more than a couple of days."

"Thank you, Mr. Bruno. I might need to speak to you again."

Aldo Bruno shrugged. When Espinosa left the room, he bumped into Mercedes.

"And?" she asked, concerned.

"And what?"

"How was he?"

"You can see for yourself, madam."

While Mercedes rushed into the room, the two terrified interns looked at Espinosa, ready to mount a defense against a possible alien attack. Nobody walked the chief out. Espinosa went down the elevator thinking that the whole office was getting stranger every time he visited. The two interns were like mute extras in a B movie, Aldo and Mercedes were the leads, and there was nobody else on the set, not a director, not a screenwriter, not a crew . . . but the set's backdrop was spectacular.

It was ten to eleven and he thought he'd walk back to the station, but at that time of day the sun was beating down on both sides of the Avenida Atlântica and he didn't feel like walking down the Avenida Copacabana, packed with people and traffic. He jumped on a bus, thinking about the main players in the story. Aldo Bruno was convincing. He was really suffering and upset about his wife's death, not just playing a role. Mercedes, too, seemed affected by Camila's death, since in her case there was a secondary benefit. She could take the place of the protector, even the provider of affection, now that the coast was clear. And she certainly had the looks to step into the leading role.

As soon as he got to the Twelfth Precinct and walked into his office, he called in Ramiro and Welber. Ramiro was the only one there: Welber was out on a job. Ramiro arrived immediately.

"Come in, Ramiro. Have a seat. I sent Welber to check out Dr. Camila's patients. He must be taking care of that. Of course the Fourteenth Precinct and Homicide are doing the same. But in our case there's a pretty odd situation. Listen closely. A murder is committed, we go out looking for clues and suspects, and in the process of so doing come across a small group of people. Two weeks later, another murder takes place with entirely different characteristics, and once again we go out looking for clues and suspects and come across a small group of people. And here's the surprise: the people we visit and interrogate in the second case are the same ones we saw and interrogated in the first, yet the crimes apparently have nothing to do with each other . . ."

"It's a pretty big coincidence."

"Exactly. The kind of coincidence I tend to mistrust. Actually, the biggest coincidence is that the same people were at both crime scenes, one of them as the victim. . . . And there's also the coincidence that the same person was the first one to get to the scene."

"What do you want me to do?"

"Find two new detectives and let them do the work you and Welber have been doing. I'm going to need you for a different job as soon as Welber brings back the information he's been gathering."

Welber didn't return until the next day, and with only part of the information. They met once again in the boss's office, and Welber told them about the information he'd gathered.

"The job seemed easy, since we had the names, the days they saw the doctor, and even their payment information, but that didn't really get me anywhere. All those things were in her agenda, but almost all the patients had only a first name. There were no addresses, and some of them didn't even have a phone number. Of course they didn't leave a photo or fill in a form like they'd do at a school or a gym. And there wasn't a file with their clinical information either. So: an agenda with a dozen names of men and women, with the phone numbers of nine of them. I talked to the doormen and all they said was that the building was one of the busiest in Ipanema. There are more than a hundred offices, many of which receive scores of clients every day. Impossible to know who's going where. The doormen know some of the people who work there, but not their clients. Of the twelve current patients, four are men and eight are women, and of the twelve, only three started this year—a dentist who also has an office in Ipanema, an artist, and a woman named Antonia; the rest have been there longer. The problem is that they almost all pay cash, so we didn't have canceled checks showing their full names, addresses, professions. The most recent patients are the two women—Maria and Antonia—who started around the same time. Maria is the artist. All I have for Antonia is her first name and contact number. On the afternoon of the murder, Camila saw four patients, all regulars. The last was Antonia, who left around six. Between the dentist and the second patient she had a one-hour interval. The autopsy established the time of death as between five and seven. Anyone could have come in during the last session or even after the last patient left. The door can be opened from the outside if it's not locked."

Welber then discussed the little he'd managed to learn about her patients. He hadn't spoken with any of them personally.

"Fine," said Espinosa. "The work you were doing with amputees will be carried on by some junior detectives. Now you need to devote yourselves to her patients. As for Aldo Bruno and Mercedes, I want them to think we're laying off them definitively . . . let their guard down . . . but I want you to keep on them the whole time, taking the utmost care not to be spotted. I know that you're good at that."

When they were leaving, he added: "I also want pictures of all of them."

PART III

It was pouring down rain when they said good-bye to the hosts. Several of the younger guests offered to get the car that was parked at the end of the street, a bit more than fifty meters from where they were standing. He thanked them, said that he'd just dart up there and that he didn't mind getting wet since they were on their way home. The host couple stood talking with his wife while he ran off. The rain, the wind, and the poor lighting interfered so much with his vision that he had to stay by the curb in order to reach his destination. The rainwater poured down the steep street, drenching his socks and shoes. An umbrella wouldn't have been much help in those circumstances. He managed to reach the car, almost running, with the key in his hand, then jerked open the door and dived inside. He wiped his face with his handkerchief and started the engine. He had to turn the car around since it was facing the end of the street.

When he turned on the lights, he could only partially make out the scene before him. The light that fell on the black rock wall met a strange tangle of vines and ferns that were being whipped around by the wind. In the middle of the ever-changing scene, a static form stood out, less than three meters in front of the car. The water pouring down the windshield almost completely blocked his vision. He turned on the windshield wipers and concentrated on the form that now presented itself in ghostly immobility. It was a man standing there, facing the car, who didn't seem to be bothered by the rain and the wind. He was wearing shorts and a T-shirt. He was standing with the help of crutches . . . he had only one leg, the other having been amputated above the knee. The man was soaking wet, his clothes sticking to his body, and he wasn't moving. Aldo looked at him without knowing if he himself had been seen, since the lights of the car were shining straight at the other man. The man inside the car jerked his face away from the window and instinctively lowered his head. The man with the crutches in the rain was Nilson. There was no doubt about it. The same long face, the same cold, defiant eyes looked at him, confronting him, more than thirty years after their first meeting.

The man inside the car couldn't take his eyes off that ghost or turn back and retreat. He thought that if he simply drove forward, Nilson wouldn't have time to get away from the car. It was the perfect moment, the one he had fantasized about for three and a half decades. He remembered the revolver in the glove compartment, which made him the absolute master of the situation. Despite all that, despite his physical superiority, he was overtaken by terror, paralyzed in front of that specter from the past.

Despite his initial certainty, he tried to convince himself that it was an optical illusion, perhaps a momentary hallucination. While he was trying to lie to himself, Nilson's right arm moved and pointed something at him. The man inside the car threw himself down, opened the glove compartment, and grabbed the revolver, but instead of sitting back down he opened the door and ran into the rain with the revolver in his hand. When he turned back to where Nilson should have been, he had already moved in reaction to the headlights. The rain was still falling with the same intensity, accompanied by the constant noise of thunder. He hadn't entirely lost sight of Nilson, but he couldn't see him as clearly as before. He could see his general shape, but he couldn't make out his movements; he couldn't even tell if he was moving or if he was standing still. There was no doubt that he was standing. The car and the lights were still on. He didn't understand how Nilson could have seen anything with the lights shining right in his eyes . . . and he didn't have any doubt that his former tormentor still had his eyes on him . . . and had recognized him. Maybe he'd already been there a long time, ever since he'd parked the car, and had sat waiting for him to return. Maybe he'd been hoping, just like Aldo himself, ever since that first encounter over three decades before, for a final, definitive conflict.

Now both were soaking wet, with the rain pouring down their hair and eyes, blurring their vision. When a series of lighting bolts illuminated the dead-end street with successive flashes, the man with the gun in his hand was momentarily blinded and lost sight of Nilson. The lights of the car were now all he had, except that Nilson was no longer there. He imagined that he was hidden on the other side of the car, or even that he had already gone down the street.

Impossible. A man with his determination wouldn't avoid a confrontation after waiting all those years in the rain.

When more lightning lit up the area, he saw Nilson only a few feet away. Without hesitating, he pointed the revolver and pressed the trigger. The sound of the shot was lost in the noise of the thunder. He quickly looked back, at the apartment building and the neighboring houses, in search of a face in a window or a person on the sidewalk, but the street was deserted and there was no light in any window. He walked around the car, got in, threw the weapon on the passenger seat, turned the car around, and drove down the street to get his wife, who was waiting at the gate of the house. He looked back in the rearview mirror to see if Nilson was still standing there, but he couldn't see anything in the complete darkness. He wasn't sure that he had aimed right and he didn't remember if Nilson had fired as well. He was sure he hadn't been injured. He didn't remember having seen Nilson fall. All he remembered was having fired. When he stopped the car to let his wife get in, he was frightened by the idea that she could sit on top of the gun. He glanced at the floor and the seats in the rear, but he didn't see the weapon. Maybe he had tossed it back in the glove compartment.

Though he drove carefully on the way down, his head was a whirlwind of images that whipped through with startling speed. He felt that all the fears he had accumulated since his first meeting with Nilson, in childhood, were resurging, indifferent to time. His wife said something about how wet he was and about the dinner, but he could barely mutter anything in response. He drove home without speaking.

Even before drying off and changing his clothes, he was assaulted by doubts about what he thought had happened. He knew for sure that he had gone to the end of the street to get the car and that it was raining a lot. He also knew that his headlights had shone on a rock wall covered with ferns and that the wind had been moving everything around. He had had some wine at dinner, and the main topic of conversation had involved a wave of attacks and urban violence. That, added to his lack of sleep and a stormy night, might have awakened dormant fantasies and delirious ideas. It wasn't the first time he'd had such a hallucination. In traumatic situations, and under the sway of intense emotions, he had sometimes seen things that turned out not to be real. It had happened a few times in his childhood and adolescence. As an adult, though, this was the first time. Except now there was another factor: the gun in the glove compartment.

His wife wasn't bothered by his silence or his mood, since he sometimes acted like that. Saying he was tired and dizzy, he managed to lie down and pretend to be sleeping without having to talk about the dinner or the other guests. His first job, as soon as he left for work in the morning, would be to get rid of the gun . . . whatever it was that had happened in the cul-de-sac.

1

He couldn't leave the kids with Camila's sister any longer—
they would feel they'd not only lost their mother but their
father as well. On the other hand, he didn't feel up to taking care of them, since he was having enough trouble taking care of himself. Of all the things that had happened
that night, including the dinner, he had an intense memory, like a mark on his body, of his finger pulling the trigger and the kick of the gun, as well as the deafening sound
of the thunderstorm echoing off the stone hill and the
sound of the wind agitating the trees. He had thought
about going back the next day to see if the shot wounded
anyone, but he was afraid of what he would find. Right
after that, the police got involved, though they hadn't
managed to figure out how it had happened nor who had
wounded whom. Aldo didn't have any doubts that he had
long wanted to kill Nilson, but he had many doubts about
whether he had managed to do so. Supposing that his shot
had missed him, Nilson could have waited for more than an
hour in the cul-de-sac, in the semihypnotic state he had
found him in, until Rogério Antunes went to get his car. . . .
Then Nilson could have surged out of the darkness, and
Rogério, thinking he was being attacked, could have shot
the supposed assailant. Then he had told the police that
the body was already on the ground when he got there; he

hadn't said anything initially so as not to get involved in an extensive and bothersome police investigation. Why couldn't that have happened? Why did he, Aldo, necessarily have to be the one who'd killed Nilson?

Now, less than a month later, Camila was dead, a death that he certainly had not desired. He'd loved his wife as he had never loved anyone, and he knew how much he would miss her, and how much their children would miss her. And the same thing that had happened in relation to Nilson's death had happened in Camila's. The only image that had stuck in his mind after opening the door was that of her nude body stretched out peacefully, as if asleep. He didn't remember anything that happened afterward. He didn't even remember opening the office door . . . couldn't say if it was locked . . . if he had the key . . . if he'd touched anything, or the body itself. Nothing. He remembered absolutely nothing. It was more than simple forgetfulness, it was a hole in his memory that could not be bridged or interpreted. At least that was how he felt in both cases. That was how he could have killed Camila without the slightest knowledge that he was doing it. The idea terrified him. Not that he believed in the least that he could have killed her—for him, that would be utterly impossible—but the gap in his memory was nearly driving him mad.

The only thing he could do to avoid drowning in that whirlpool was to dedicate himself heart and soul to his work. He had new projects that needed to be developed, and the original design work, before the detailing, was his alone. Mercedes was good for the next phases, but she wasn't experienced enough to deal with getting the project off the ground. The more time he spent at the office, the less time he had to spend at home surrounded by the memory of Camila on every side. When the kids came home, he would try to find a full-time babysitter or nanny. It wasn't a pleasant idea, but he couldn't think of a better solution.

A week after Camila's death, he was living with a jumble of images and thoughts. Every morning, those were the first that came to his mind when he awoke abruptly and totally, and they were the last things that occurred to him before he went to sleep at night.

He got to the office early. The beach was still empty of bathers and there were no traffic jams heading downtown. The pleasant temperature and the smooth ocean calmed him . . . but not for long. He sat on the window seat and started some sketches that turned into preliminary drawings. When Mercedes and the interns got there, they found several pages full of designs, indications, and notes referring to their new projects. Mercedes, the first to arrive, kissed him lovingly, which gratified his senses but confused his sentiments. Mercedes noticed the ambiguous reaction . . . and he noticed that she noticed. He worked the whole day without a break. At lunchtime he stopped only to eat a sandwich he'd ordered over the phone. At the end of the afternoon, Mercedes suggested that they go to the apartment Luíza had left for them. Aldo gave the excuse that he had to pick up the kids at his sister-in-law's house and take them home, and said that the next day he would be getting in a bit later because he had to interview a nanny.

It was extremely difficult to be back home with the kids and without Camila. None of the three spoke of her, but they all thought about her constantly. When Aldo saw it was impossible to escape the presence-absence of Camila, he took advantage of a moment when the kids were playing in their room to sit down on the floor with them and suggest that they talk about their mother. They spoke of her until late in the night, then, exhausted, fell asleep on the carpet. The next morning, they had breakfast together and sat waiting for the nanny. Cíntia and Fernando wanted to know why it couldn't be Ana, the babysitter who usually looked after them.

"Because Ana's in school and can't be with you full-time, but I promise that on the nanny's days off I'll call Ana to be with you."

The doorman rang up to say that Isabela had arrived.

Finding Camila Bruno's patients was easier than it might have been because two different precincts were working on the case and the bosses of both stations were cooperating. Even so, three patients still hadn't been located. The police had only their first names. No description, no checking account or credit card number, nothing to help identify them. All three paid every month in cash. It seemed the only way to find them would be if they voluntarily sought out the police. But why would they do that? As for the widower Aldo Bruno and his partner Mercedes, they hadn't done anything suspicious at the beginning of the investigation. Meanwhile, the examination of hospital files in search of amputees was moving along, and the detectives had found a number of viable possibilities.

Two things were especially interesting to Espinosa. The first was his conviction that the two deaths were related; the second was the question of why Camila Bruno had been found naked in her office.

Of course, the second topic was much more objective than the first. She had in fact been found naked on the couch in her office. One question was: Had she herself taken her clothes off or had she been stripped by some-. one else? Another question: Had she been stripped before or after her death? If it had happened afterward, what had been the criminal's intention? Was it a kind of postmortem exhibitionism? Sexual perversion knows no bounds, Espinosa thought.

It was nighttime, and Espinosa was thinking freely. Sometimes the flow of ideas produced an interesting theory. He wasn't worried about thinking with any logical rigor, if only because he doubted that his ideas had, at any point in his life, stemmed from any logical rigor. What he was doing was removing the pretense of logic and letting the monsters come to the surface. Some of those monsters would get sent back into the pit, but others merited closer examination. And that was a technique in which madness could be as useful as reason.

It was obvious that the murderer wanted to show off Camila's nude body in its serene beauty, without marks of violence, not even having been used sexually. The murderer had set up a perverse Sleeping Beauty scenario. The question was: Why go to the trouble? For the police? For her husband? For her patients? The clue that it was meant as a scene was the absence of the sexual act (or at least of sexual penetration). Now what? What did the murderer hope to achieve with this scene?

The scene could suggest, Espinosa kept thinking, that Camila's nudity was available without physical violence. The idea wasn't entirely true, since the drug that had put her to sleep was itself a form of physical violence. Unless the murderer was only interested in the aesthetic, rather than the ethical, aspects. But what did that suggest? That Dr. Camila stripped for just anyone? Crazy. He himself had been with her twice in that office and she had never acted like anything other than a therapist and the wife of Aldo Bruno. So what was the point? To sully her image? Or just to show that Camila was stretched out nude on the sofa? Alone? No, of course, Espinosa kept thinking, it wasn't suicide. There was at least one person with whom she got naked in that office. Probably the same person who killed her.

Lately Espinosa often ended up sitting in his rocking chair at night to read, only to drift away into endless musings. He looked at the table next to him, where the three books he'd bought before his first visit to Camila's office

rested. He picked them up, read the flaps of all three, then
started reading the one on the top of the pile.

The next three days were dedicated to identifying
and locating Camila Bruno's patients. Espinosa thought it
unlikely that an ex-patient from a few years back would
wait so long to reappear and kill Camila. There was no
extra appointment in the agenda, which suggested that the
murderer had taken her by surprise. Ramiro and Welber
focused on the current patients. They also kept track of
Aldo and Mercedes because of the closeness Espinosa had
noted between them.

As for the hospital files, they were also nearing the
end of the project to identify the homeless man. They'd
whittled it down to a small number of cases, and now they
just had to sift carefully through them.

That was where the two investigations stood on Friday
afternoon, which was calm enough for Espinosa to call
Irene and invite her to spend the weekend with him . . .
"Your place or mine, whatever you prefer."

"You know I always prefer yours," she said. "We can
make a bigger mess there."

Over breakfast on Saturday morning, Espinosa outlined
his most important plans for the apartment, including con-
structing wooden shelving for his books, fixing the toaster,
and having the loose tiles on the floor repaired.

"You didn't include fumigating for the ants."

"They've already been decimated . . . or expelled, I'm not sure which."

"Do you think it's possible to take your so-called problems seriously?"

"But they are problems!"

"Of course, hon, but if you ever decide to accept a foreign object in this apartment, I'll buy you the best toaster I can find."

"As long as you let the old toaster stay. You know . . . I could need it."

"You love that old, broken toaster more than you love me."

"But of course!"

Irene placed her hand on the toaster and stood up from the table. Espinosa felt a chill in his gut imagining where she was going to toss the thing.

"Irene, what are you going . . ."

Irene went into the bedroom . . . Espinosa followed her to the doorway. . . . The toaster was on top of the bed.

"Let's do it this way. You screw the toaster and tell me if it was better than with me. If you want, I'll plug it in for you."

Irene said this while entirely naked, standing beside the bed, pointing at the toaster. Espinosa walked into the bedroom, grabbed Irene around her waist, and took her into the living room.

"Espinosa! What are you doing?"

"Since you put the toaster in bed, I'm going to put you on the table. . . . And I don't even need to plug you in."

It was two in the afternoon and they were choosing a nice place to have lunch when the phone rang. Espinosa had no idea who could be calling at that hour on a Saturday.

"Chief, it's Welber."

"What happened?"

"Aldo and Mercedes entered an apartment in Copacabana at ten-fifteen last night and just left now, holding hands until they walked out of the building. It's a small residential building on a side street in Copacabana. It's not her address. I took a picture of the two leaving the building. It came out nicely."

"Good work. You can go home now."

Aldo didn't feel right walking through Copacabana on a Saturday afternoon in the company of a woman like Mercedes, who attracted the attention of both men and women. He would rather not have gone out with her the night before. He thought it was too early. Less than two weeks. And now here he was, walking arm in arm with a pretty young woman . . . twenty years younger . . . in broad daylight, on the busiest street in Copacabana. They could have at least been a bit more discreet. But Mercedes always ended up convincing him that there was nothing wrong, that he wasn't offending the memory of his ex-wife, that it wasn't anything against Camila (even if only because she was dead) or against her memory, but something *for* her,

Mercedes, who had nothing to do with Camila, who didn't even know her personally. . . . And it was true that it had been a great night. Mercedes was young, very pretty, decisive, and there was no question that she was helping him out of his depression. Cíntia and Fernando had never seen Mercedes, they didn't even know what she looked like. But Aldo thought it was only a question of time before some resentful busybody made sure they found out that their father was dating another woman. Some friend or even a relative of Camila's could surprise them at that hour in Copacabana. That wouldn't be good. And it would look very bad if it got back to Chief Espinosa, whose greatest pleasure of the last few weeks had been seeking him out for apparently innocent conversations. Apparently. The man must have been a failure in life, and now he got off on little power games, and took every chance to invade people's privacy and threaten them. It wouldn't be good if Espinosa found out about his affair with Mercedes. Besides, it wasn't even clear that it amounted to an affair. She certainly thought it did. More than once she had said that when Luíza got back from her trip they would have to find a place of their own, not something borrowed, provisional. Mercedes wanted something definitive. . . . If it wasn't provisional, it was definitive. . . . What was she thinking? That they'd get married? That was a little hasty. Hasty and presumptuous. After all, he had never suggested any such possibility. Of course he felt proud to have a woman as attractive as Mercedes, but that didn't give her license . . .

"What are you thinking about?" Mercedes asked, her hand on his arm.

"Nothing important."

"But your crinkled forehead suggests otherwise. Don't forget that you have every right to happiness and pleasure."

"I know I do."

"So? What's standing in your way? The past?"

"The past is still the present, Mercedes."

"And do the kids worry you?"

"Of course they worry me. Losing your mother at age eight or nine is terrible."

"If you want, I can take them out to get their minds off of it."

"Thanks, but that won't be necessary. I got a kind of nanny for them. Her name is Isabela. She seems nice and good at her job. They're spending their first weekend together. I hope it works out."

"Is she pretty?"

"What kind of a question is that, Mercedes? She's a girl."

"How old is she?"

"What?"

"Twenty? Twenty-five?"

"Sorry, Mercedes, I forget you aren't even thirty. Yes, she's pretty. But she can't hold a candle to you. She's simply pretty, but you're much more than that."

"How much more?"

"You're sensual, charming, intelligent, understanding, decisive, efficient."

"It sounds like you're describing a businesswoman. All you need to do is add that I speak English, French, and Spanish."

"What do you want me to say?"

"It's not what I want you to say. It's what you want to say."

"I want to say that you're hot."

"You could have started there: hot, beautiful, sensual, et cetera."

The building was on Rua Leopoldo Miguez, a little street parallel to the Avenida Copacabana, discreet and quiet, but only a block from the two busiest streets in the neighborhood. Mercedes was clearly proud of the first night they had spent together. She had managed to bring about a change in Aldo, taking him from melancholy to mania— at least sexually. With time, anything was possible. Quick encounters at the end of the afternoon were one thing, fast sex with a hint of adventure; a whole night together was something else entirely, without having to run back home, a night that could blend into the next day without physical or temporal limits. She was happy with the success of her plan. It was exclusively up to her to transform the arrangement into something permanent.

As they walked, Aldo worried about the people around them. A few more steps to the Avenida Copacabana, and there it would be impossible to walk two blocks without running into some acquaintance of his or Camila's. Mercedes didn't seem to think that mattered in the least; she had a young person's freedom and daring—a young person who had not yet established definitive ties, which was a bit surprising for such a beautiful woman. When they got to the corner, Aldo managed to untangle their arms and they started walking side by side like two colleagues. Mercedes took the snub in stride. After that, they would walk in opposite directions. Mercedes would head to the left and Aldo to the right, toward Ipanema. . . . Unless they kept walking together in whatever direction they chose, as she hoped would happen. But it didn't. Aldo claimed he had to be with his children on their first weekend home without their mother. He hailed a taxi and offered to drop Mercedes at her apartment, but she declined.

Aldo thought he could have lunch with the kids and, now, with Isabela too. The nanny's parents were from northern Italy, and with her blond hair and blue eyes she looked more German than Italian. Aldo was happy when he opened the door and heard the kids laughing at something she had said. Isabela was cheerful and tactful, a perfect combination for what he thought the kids needed. He didn't know what would happen over the course of time. The nanny seemed like the best solution for the first months after Camila's death, but he didn't know if it was the best thing over the long term. He was open to the possibility of remarrying; he couldn't imagine being alone for the rest of his life. He was also open to the possibility that his future wife would get along so well with the kids that he wouldn't need a nanny, be it Isabela or anyone else. The idea that this future wife could be Mercedes was seductive but problematic, especially because it was a relationship that had transformed from a professional one into a personal one—but also because that transformation had happened before Camila's death. It was one thing to be an occasional lover and quite another to take the place that Camila had occupied.

Isabela slept in the room next to the kids' room, which had originally been intended as an office or guest room but had never ended up being either one. For the first time it would have an actual use. As for Aldo, he stayed in the master bedroom, sleeping in the same bed he had shared with Camila for ten years.

Monday morning began hot and rainy, but with promising news. Espinosa was greeted in his office with a photograph on top of his desk of Aldo and Mercedes walking out of a building arm in arm. The picture, taken with a telephoto lens from inside a car parked on the opposite curb, showed both faces clearly. The other news was that one of the informants tasked to find Joca, the former club employee who was friends with Skinny, had tracked him down. Joca was working as a cleaner in a building in Ipanema and slept at his workplace, which was why he was no longer spotted in the Pavão-Pavãozinho slum.

"What are we going to do about the relationship between Aldo and Mercedes?" Welber asked. "Neither of them broke the law by spending the night together. I'd say that they were a little hasty, at most."

"The question is: Were they too hasty, or had this already been going on?"

"You think they were already sleeping together before the doctor's death?"

"I think so."

"And do you think they could have . . ."

"I think that would be absurd and completely unnecessary."

"But not impossible," Ramiro added. "So what are we going to do?"

"Investigate the couple's movements on the day of the crime, even though I think that if they were already lovers before the death, there would be no reason to kill her. But first I want you two to go to the building where Joca works and show him the picture of Skinny that we did with the computer. If it's a positive ID, get as much information as you can about the victim. You can do that this morning. Meanwhile, I'm going to chat with Aldo Bruno."

2

It was ten-fifteen when Espinosa got to Aldo Bruno's office. He learned from the doorman that the four employees had gotten there before ten, all around the same time. Espinosa didn't notify them that he was coming up, and he hadn't called ahead. As on his previous visit, Mercedes opened the door.

"Officer!"

"I know it's not the best surprise on a Monday morning, Mercedes, but it's my job. Almost always unwelcome."

"What can I do for you, sir?"

"I'd like to come in, if you don't mind. . . . Then, I'd like to talk to Mr. Bruno, if he can see me."

"Come in, please. I'll tell him you're here."

Aldo's door was closed and Espinosa didn't see the two interns, which led him to suppose that they'd all been in a meeting when he'd arrived. Mercedes and the interns exited and Aldo appeared at the door of his office, inviting Espinosa to come in.

"Good morning, Officer. What's going on?"

"Same as usual, Mr. Bruno, details. All we do is chase down details. I already told you that our work isn't just tracking down criminals, it's also making sure that innocent people are not unjustly accused."

"That's good to hear, sir."

"But that part of the job can be as unpleasant and tiresome as finding the guilty party. Especially when the person being investigated is linked to two homicides. So I ask you to be patient with me."

"In fact, my name isn't linked to two homicides. I just found the victims, one of whom was my own wife."

"That's why I say your name is linked to the deaths. I didn't say how."

"Fine, Officer. How can I help you?"

"By telling me in detail what you did on the evening when your wife was killed."

Aldo's posture changed. His body tensed, his jaw flexed, his voice lowered, and the rhythm of his voice became slower and more careful.

"In detail?"

"If you can. We can start, for example, with lunchtime."

"Fine. I went out around one and ate at a Japanese restaurant here on this block."

"Alone?"

"Yes. My colleagues had gone earlier. We rarely all go out together. I was back before two, and I only left again at around five-thirty, more or less."

"Is that when you usually go home?"

"Usually it's a bit later, but on that day I wanted to stop by a store in Ipanema to buy some clothes."

"What kind of clothes?"

"Short-sleeved shirts and T-shirts, for the summer."

"Do you know the name of the shop, and did you keep the receipts?"

"The name of the shop, of course; it's where I always buy clothes. But I threw away the receipts—I don't usually keep them. I left the store around seven and went home. All on foot. Whenever I can, I walk to work. Three kilometers each way, it's my exercise. And I also try to get home before dinner so I can see my kids."

"You went straight home from the store?"

"That's right. It's very close."

"And you didn't go out again?"

"Not until I went to Camila's office, worried that she was late and hadn't called."

"What time was that?"

"Nine, as I already told you. I tried the doorknob and the door opened. There's a little waiting room, and through there was where she saw her patients. The door to her office was closed. When I opened it, I could see the whole scene. . . . And I was immediately sure that Camila was dead."

"Why were you so sure? Did you check if she was breathing, or if she had a pulse?"

"Officer, when I touched her, her body was cold. There was no sign of life. It was obvious that she was dead."

"Thank you, Mr. Bruno. Now I'd like to talk to Mercedes."

"Mercedes? Yes . . . sure. . . . She's next door."

Mercedes had a desk in the main room, where the two interns also worked. When Espinosa appeared, she sat up as if waiting to be called in for a conversation.

"Is there anywhere we can speak in private?" Espinosa asked.

"Sure. There's another office we use when we need more architects or interns."

The office, a former bedroom, faced the inside of the building, but it was roomy and pleasant. There was a round table with several chairs around it, where the two sat down. Mercedes was on the defensive, which she showed by using few gestures or words.

"Before we start, a question: Did you know Dr. Camila?"

"No. I don't think she ever came by the office in all the time I've worked here."

"I can imagine that for all of you, not just for Mr. Bruno, the day of her death must have left a strong impression. It was at the end of the afternoon, last Tuesday. I'd like for you to tell me in as much detail as possible everything you did that afternoon."

"May I ask why?"

"Because I need to know."

"Okay. Starting at what time?"

"Starting at lunchtime."

"We went out for lunch at noon . . ."

"Sorry. Who's 'we'?"

"Rafaela, Henrique, and I."

Espinosa nodded and indicated that she could continue.

"We went to a buffet-style place nearby. We were back before one. Aldo was waiting for us to get back before he left himself."

"Why didn't he go with you?"

"So that the office wouldn't be empty. We're working on two projects and we get calls from construction companies, contractors, workmen. . . . And we don't have a secretary. . . . That's how we decided to do it."

"Go on, please."

"At four-thirty I went to my analyst."

"Can you confirm that?"

"Of course."

"Where is your analyst's office?"

"Right here in Copacabana."

"After your analysis, where did you go?"

"Home. I live in Copacabana. Almost all my life unfolds in this neighborhood."

"You didn't leave home again after that?"

"No."

"Can someone confirm that?"

"I don't think so. . . . Maybe the doorman of my building."

"When did you hear about the death of Dr. Camila?"

"The next day, when I got to work. Rafaela and Henrique told me, but they didn't know that she'd been murdered. We only heard that in the afternoon, when we talked to Aldo on the phone."

"Thank you, Mercedes. We might need to come back to speak to you again."

"May I ask a question, Officer?"

"Go ahead."

"Why me?"

"What do you mean?"

"There's three of us in the office, besides Aldo. Why am I the only one being questioned?"

"Because the other two aren't sleeping with Mr. Bruno."

As soon as Espinosa got into the elevator, Mercedes ran to tell Aldo what the policeman had said. She was a bit nervous and scared. Aldo made her repeat the entire conversation, which she did almost verbatim.

"I told you we were moving too fast," Aldo said as soon as he heard Mercedes's story.

"Too fast in relation to what? Weren't we already screwing before Camila's death? And even if we hadn't been, does the fact that a man's wife dies mean he can never have sex again? But more than that, what do the cops have to do with the fact that we spent the night together? Is that against the law now?"

Mercedes had gone from being nervous and scared to furious indignation.

"What kind of country is this, where a man and a woman can't spend the night together? Is there some legal or religious law against it?"

"It's not legal or religious, Mercedes, it's moral."

"Moral?! What the fuck is this morality that says it's fine to cheat on your wife when she's alive but not when she's dead? Cheating in memoriam? Did you throw an orgy in memory of your wife?! Were we at a bacchanal ten days after she died?"

"It was too soon, Mercedes."

"Soon? So tell me, how long do you have to wait, in your moral opinion?"

"It's a question of feeling . . . and common sense . . ."

"Feeling and common sense? When we were fucking right here in the office, in this very room, and when we were happily fucking in my friend's apartment, there was no feeling or common sense? It wasn't early or late, Aldo, it was when we decided to do it. . . . Our desires decided it was time. That's the law. That's the morality."

The rain that began that morning had stopped and the weather was slightly overcast and hot. Espinosa thought he'd still have to wait a few months before the heat got a bit less Amazonian. Sixty-eight or seventy degrees was a civilized temperature. It didn't have to be less than that: just enough so that he could walk to the corner, or up or down a few stairs, without breaking out in sweat. And now, leaving Aldo's office building, he wondered whether he should walk back to the station or take an air-conditioned bus. Since it wasn't too sunny, he decided to walk back down the Avenida Atlântica. The view was beautiful, in sun or rain. While he walked down the sidewalk, he imagined Mercedes and Aldo discussing his comment. Nothing like stirring up the waters to get at the mud on the bottom, he thought. Instead of going straight to the station, he went to the Italian place where he often had lunch. He got there right when the regular customers were taking their places.

He managed to snag one of the last tables. Out of habit, he accepted the owner's daily suggestion.

Ramiro and Welber returned satisfied from their meeting with Joca. He'd immediately recognized the picture of Skinny, and when Espinosa came back from lunch, the two were meeting with the detectives in charge of examining amputees' medical records, comparing the facts gleaned from the janitor with those they had already compiled.

"Chief, we've already found the file with the amputation. There's no police record. The amputation wasn't the result of police action. It was gangrene. The victim didn't have a record. The surgery occurred when he was thirty years old. He lived in Maricá, in the Lake Region, and had never been in Rio before the surgery. He stayed here awhile, after he was released from the hospital. He spent a short time in a shack in the Pavão-Pavãozinho slum, but he couldn't pay his rent and went back to Maricá, where his wife and kids lived. After that, he used his medical record to get further treatment. He was never really homeless—rather, he only slept in the streets when he came to Rio looking for work or medical treatment."

"Did you get the address in Maricá?"

"We did."

"Send a telegram reporting his death. Say that if any relative wants information about the circumstances of his death, they should look for us here at the station. Also send it to the precinct in Maricá. By the way, what was his name?"

"Elias do Nascimento."

"One more thing, Chief. We got pictures of almost all of Dr. Camila's patients. The only ones missing are the two new women, whom we haven't found. They're digital photos, and we sent all of them to your computer. There are printed pictures on your desk, if you want to use them."

"Very good. Let's show the pictures to the doormen and the elevator operators in her building. And now that we know who Skinny really was, let's see if we can figure out who killed him."

Espinosa was convinced that the nudity of Camila Bruno was the key to figuring out why she was murdered and the sign that would reveal the criminal's identity, just like he was convinced that Camila's murderer was someone she'd known. That's why the pictures were so important. Doctors' patients show up once or twice a year, but therapists see their patients regularly—once, twice, or three times a week, and they end up knowing the doormen and the elevator operators. Aldo said he hadn't been in her office more than a couple of times in the last few years. He was certainly unknown to the building's staff.

The rest of the day was difficult and unpleasant for Aldo. Mercedes had retreated to her desk, refusing to speak to him even when it was about business. The two interns, Rafaela and Henrique, realized that something serious had happened, but they didn't have any idea what. All they knew was that it had something to do with the policeman's visit. They didn't want to ask Mercedes about it because she was in such a bad mood, and they didn't dare ask Aldo Bruno. Except to say that they were going to lunch, none of the four said more than a couple of words until the end of the afternoon, when they all left.

Aldo was the last to leave, and started heading home. He hadn't gone half a block when he felt someone walking alongside him. It was Mercedes. At first she said nothing, striding silently alongside him until the end of the block. Aldo didn't understand. If she had been waiting to accompany him, she must have something to say. It was clear enough that she didn't intend to walk silently all the way through Ipanema. They crossed the street, and when they made it to the next corner Aldo broke the silence.

"How am I supposed to interpret this scene?"

"I was hoping for something better from you than that. This morning I talked the whole time. Now it's your turn."

"Why do you think I have to say something?"

"Don't you? What did you lose? Your voice or your mind?"

"I don't need to justify myself to you."

"You don't? Is that how you treated your wife? Sex without conversation? Or was it conversation without sex?"

Aldo spun around and grabbed her shoulder as if he was going to attack her. Mercedes broke away and said:

"Couldn't have been sex or conversation."

She turned away.

"When you want both of those things with me, for longer than just a quickie, come find me. I quit as of now. Good-bye."

Aldo kept walking, but more slowly, as if those two blocks had consumed all the energy he had planned to expend on getting home. He was too tired to continue, and he didn't want to get a taxi. He went into a bar to have a coffee while he let the emotion—he didn't know if it was love or hatred—cool off. The immediate cause of what was happening wasn't anything he'd done or not done, but the constant intrusions of Chief Espinosa and his assistants. Obviously, they had been watching him and Mercedes twenty-four hours a day, so that they could later show up in the office with vague, threatening questions. There was no doubt that Chief Espinosa could get under his skin, and everything indicated that he was doing the same with Mercedes. The officer didn't seem like he was in a hurry—he could keep going long enough to drive Aldo to desperation. If that was the game he wanted to play, Aldo would play. From then on he would be as economical as possible in his answers, saying the bare minimum, or maybe nothing at all. Espinosa's activities would be cut short when he stopped feeding them with his words.

It took Aldo almost twice as long as usual to get home. His legs hurt, possibly a mix of tension and fatigue, he thought. He talked with the kids and Isabela, sat in his room for a while, and went into the living room to make himself a whiskey. He needed a bit to relax. He drank one more, and then another. The maid announced that dinner was ready. Even with dinner, the drink made its effects known. It helped him relax, but it also brought up scenes of Chief Espinosa asking questions about the deaths of Nilson and Camila. He had one more drink, which made him extremely sleepy. He fell asleep on the living room sofa and only got up at daybreak, feeling bad, nauseous, wanting to throw up, and with a throbbing headache. He couldn't lie down. He took an aspirin and sat waiting for the sun to come up. Only then did he nod off a bit, still seated. He was awakened by the children, who were scared to find their father still wearing the clothes he'd had on the night before, sitting in the living room, visibly in bad condition. Isabela asked if he was feeling all right and if he needed help. He said that he just needed to wash his face and that he'd have breakfast with them.

Even after his breakfast and extended bath, the bad feeling he'd had the night before persisted. It wasn't just a physical feeling, it was also the feeling of being invaded by a kind of idea-virus that was spreading and growing with each passing day, leaving him in a state of terrible vulnerability.

He went to work wondering if Mercedes was serious about her decision to leave the office—and, of course, him. She was impulsive and possessive as a lover, but she was a good worker. He'd miss both sides of her. He took a cab. He was in a hurry. The first thing he did when he got in was examine Mercedes's desk to see if she'd removed her belongings. There were no personal items on the desk, and the drawers were locked. If she'd left, she wouldn't have locked the drawers . . . unless she'd given the key to Rafaela or Henrique . . . or left them with the doorman: that would be even more impersonal. He checked his office for a letter or even for the keys, but there was nothing. The only sign of her departure was the absence of visible personal posses- sions, and even that was not a reliable indicator, because those could be in the drawers. He'd have to wait and see. He waited in vain until the evening.

Mercedes had decided not to show up that day and, depending on Aldo's reaction—which she would learn from Rafaela and Henrique—also not to show up on the days thereafter. She wanted Aldo to miss her before she would hint at a possible return. Aldo wasn't the kind of man who could live without a woman by his side, a woman to help him through his emotional crises. She knew that because she'd been working side by side with him ever since she'd started there, and she also knew it because of the little facts about his personal history that he'd dribbled out during lunches, relaxed moments in the office, and, lately, in bed. Lots of the comments he'd made referred to the period just before his marriage, pointing out just how much Camila had helped him professionally and emotion- ally, giving him strength and confidence. Now he didn't have Camila, he didn't have any close friends who could help him, he wasn't religious, and he was about to lose the only source of physical contact and emotional support he had—both of which, moreover, were of outstanding quality: Mercedes. It was Tuesday, she could take a night bus to São Paulo and get there early Wednesday morning, just in time to have breakfast in Vila Madalena with a friend of hers from college. She'd done that before. Julia lived alone in a little house, but it was big enough to shelter her until the weekend.

3

Wednesday. Espinosa had breakfast thinking about the visit he would pay to Aldo and Mercedes. Perhaps the last. It was time to move from these brief conversations to depositions at the station: a drastic change in procedure and venue. The advantage of informal visits was that they didn't have forewarning or lawyers; it was a friendly way to get information, allowing the investigator to follow up on unusual leads without the fear of illegality. The interrogation performed at the station was more intimidating, but on the other hand it had to obey certain clearly established procedures. Naturally, the person could refuse to be interviewed by the police in their home or workplace without a lawyer present, but in general most people acquiesced, viewing those encounters as solely intended to gather information.

That's why Espinosa preferred, one more time, to visit Aldo and Mercedes instead of calling them down to the station. As always, he arrived unannounced. He thought it was odd that Mercedes didn't open the door. Henrique, a bit awkward and unsure about whether to invite the officer in or to tell Mr. Bruno first, ended up moving aside to allow Espinosa to enter.

"Good morning, Officer."

3

3

"Good morning, Henrique. That's your name, right?"

"Yes, sir. . . . Just a minute, I'm going to tell Mr. Bruno you're here."

Espinosa looked around and only saw Rafaela, the other intern. The door of Aldo Bruno's office was open, and all he heard were the voices of Henrique and Aldo. No sign of Mercedes. It was ten in the morning. Aldo came back with the intern.

"Good morning, Officer."

"Good morning, Mr. Bruno. Sorry I didn't call ahead."

"No problem. Come on in."

They went into the architect's office and closed the door behind them.

"First off, Mr. Bruno, I've tried to get in touch with Mercedes and discovered that I don't have her home number."

"She doesn't have a land line. She uses her cell phone." He wrote the number on a piece of paper and passed it to Espinosa. "I've also been trying to get in touch with her since last night; she apparently has her phone off."

"That's the advantage of a cell phone."

"Maybe, but a land line can be turned off too."

"And do you think there's any reason why she would have her phone off?"

"I don't know, Officer. I just know that she should be here this morning."

"Did something happen? A fight . . ."

"Officer Espinosa . . ."

"Mr. Bruno, it's just us here in this room. I know you two

are having an affair. I don't have anything against any-body's personal life, unless, of course, it interferes with my police work."

"How is it interfering with your work?"

"I'm still not entirely sure, which is why I'd like to speak with Mercedes, and that was one of the reasons I came here."

"Well, then, Officer, we're in the same boat. I'm looking for her as well."

"Except that we're not in the same boat."

"Just an expression, sir. Of course not. You said that was one of the reasons you came here this morning. May I ask what the other was?"

"The other is to ask a question that in fact has already been asked, except that, since the situation has changed, I need to ask again."

Espinosa didn't ask immediately. First, he looked at Aldo Bruno for two seconds.

"What question?" he said, hesitantly.

"Did you know or had you ever seen Elias do Nasci-mento?"

"Who?"

"Elias do Nascimento."

"I've never heard of him. Who is he?"

"The homeless man who was murdered on Mascarenhas de Moraes."

"Elias do Nascimento? But . . . but . . ."

"Yes?"

"That wasn't his name."

"What do you mean? Did you know him?"

"No, but someone had given another name."

"Who?"

"I don't remember . . . one of the policemen . . . or one of the employees . . . I can't remember."

"His name is Elias do Nascimento. Definitely. He lived in Maricá and he came to Rio for treatment in the Hospital Miguel Couto, where his leg was amputated because of gangrene."

"Maricá? He wasn't a homeless person who lived in Copacabana? That's what you told me."

"Because we still didn't have his medical records. He was only homeless on the days when he was in Rio for medical treatment. Then he went back to Maricá, where he lived with his family."

"With his family?"

"Yes. Is there a problem?"

"No . . . I must have misunderstood."

"What do you think you misunderstood?"

"I thought the police knew who he was."

"In fact we only found out who he was after we examined all the records of leg amputations in public hospitals over the last twenty years. We examined hundreds of records, until we found his."

"And there's no doubt about the identification?"

"None. He was identified by his family. On the medical form, instead of a signature there was a fingerprint. You seem to have known the victim."

"Certainly not. Maybe the missing leg reminded me of some amputee I might have seen on the street."

"Okay. Anyway, the case is still ongoing. We've discovered the identity of the dead man, but we still need to discover who killed him."

Espinosa took the piece of paper where Aldo had written Mercedes's phone number, said good-bye to the architect, and walked to the door. He stopped halfway, turned around, and sat back down.

"There's one more question I can't get out of my mind, Mr. Bruno. I know it's an extremely delicate matter, but I have to ask you. In my opinion, the nudity of your wife's body had nothing to do with a presumed sexual aggression. That's already been more than confirmed. I suppose that the murderer was trying to send a message to someone. And that's my question: Do you have any idea what the message was and for whom it was meant?"

"Why do you think it was a message?"

"Because it was so ostentatious. It wasn't the nudity of someone who was changing clothes and was surprised by an attacker; it was an arranged nudity, a kind of scene, something meant to be seen by someone else."

"What happened is completely absurd—none of it makes sense. Her death doesn't make sense, the way it happened doesn't make sense, her nudity doesn't make sense. Nothing makes sense. And then to think that the murderer was sending someone a message . . . it's too much for me."

"I don't think they killed your wife just to send a message, but I do think that they might have decided to send a message after they committed the crime. If we consider that the person was someone she knew, the possibilities are relatively limited."

"The only thing that occurs to me is that it was some patient who went crazy. . . . I can't imagine any friend or acquaintance doing something like that."

"We're investigating the patients, but we haven't been able to find two women, Maria and Antonia. Do you know who they are?"

"Camila rarely spoke about what happened in her practice, and when she did she didn't name names."

"Thank you, Mr. Bruno. I'll leave you to get back to work in peace."

"To work, definitely, but in peace . . . ?"

Espinosa, Welber, and Ramiro printed copies of all the photographs of Camila's patients, friends, and acquaintances that they had managed to get their hands on. It wasn't much, but it did make a nice private archive, as they themselves called it, and the "private" referred both to Camila's personal relationships and to her patients. They would start out with the doormen, parking lot attendants, and elevator operators, and then would move on to her neighbors in her office building.

They had decided to do it in the afternoon, because that was when the doctor usually saw her patients. There was a greater chance that the employees would be the same ones who were working that day. At the reception area, there was a doorman and an assistant and, just in front of them, there was a man in a suit and dark glasses, obviously the security guard, who moved forward when he saw the policemen arrive.

A wide marble counter separated the doormen from the public. After identifying himself and introducing his assistants, Espinosa asked the two doormen:

"Do you two work here on weekday afternoons?"

"Yes," answered the one who seemed to be senior.

"And you both knew Dr. Camila Bruno, from suite 1210?"

"That's right."

"Very good. We're going to show you some pictures, about fifteen, almost all of her patients, and I want you to tell me if any of them were here on the day she was killed, between five in the afternoon and eight at night. Take your time, look carefully—we're not in a hurry. We'll talk to you one at a time so the other can keep an eye on reception."

The senior doorman stood behind the counter, ready to begin. Espinosa started with pictures of the patients. The doorman immediately remembered three of them as having been there on that Wednesday afternoon, which his assistant confirmed, but they said that there were two other patients whose pictures weren't among those the officers displayed. Neither of them remembered exactly in what order the people in the photos had arrived, but they were almost sure that none of them had arrived at the end of the afternoon.

"Our shift is from two to eight. There's a man, big and fat, who comes twelve to one, but he's the only one here at that time; the others always start at two. The doctor worked until six or seven, never later."

"Let's continue. Now I'm going to add some pictures of the doctor's friends and acquaintances. I want you to tell me if any of these people were here that day."

Espinosa once again spread out the pictures on the counter, mixing in new ones they had not yet seen. When they showed the picture of Aldo with Mercedes leaving the building in Copacabana, the head doorman said immediately:

"There she is. She was the last one to leave."

"Who?" Espinosa asked.

"The patient who wasn't in the other pictures."

"But she's not a patient."

"Of course she is. She comes twice a week."

"And the man next to her, do you know who that is?"

"Yes. That's the doctor's husband. He never came here. I know he was her husband because he was the one who came down to say she was dead."

"This girl with him," Espinosa said, "works with him. She's an architect, not a patient of Dr. Bruno's."

Ramiro and Welber came closer to listen in on the conversation. The other doorman agreed with what his colleague was saying.

"She is a patient, sir; she always came at the end of the afternoon. She was the last one that afternoon."

"Are you sure about what you're saying? You're sure that the girl in this picture is, or was, Dr. Bruno's patient?"

"Well, sir, at least she came twice a week and stayed up there for an hour, just like the others, so she could only be a patient."

Espinosa, Welber, and Ramiro looked, astonished, at the picture and at the doormen.

"Maria or Antonia, one of the two, one of the ones whose picture we don't have. Did any of you bring a copy of the doctor's schedule?"

"I did," said Welber, "but I left it in the car. I'll go get it."

While he was looking for the agenda, Espinosa and Ramiro tried to get more details about the patient's arrival that afternoon: if she had come in just once or if she had come back afterward at another time; if she came alone; if she had ever come with the doctor's husband . . .

Welber returned almost running, with the agenda open in his hands, saying:

"Antonia! She's Antonia."

"You mean that Antonia and Mercedes are the same person . . ."

The doormen didn't know whether to be happy to have helped out in a way they couldn't quite determine or if they should worry about the consequences of their contribution. Espinosa put them at ease.

"Thank you. You have been a great deal of help. Detective Welber will take your names and your work numbers. Afterward we're going to need to take your depositions. Don't worry, we won't interfere with your work."

On the sidewalk, the three didn't know what to think about what they'd just discovered. They walked silently toward Prasa Nossa Senhora da Paz, each one lost in his own thoughts. When they got to the square, they sat on one of the benches. Espinosa was the first to speak:

"We have two surprising facts, and both of them are disturbing. The first is the discovery that Antonia, Dr. Camila's patient, and Mercedes, the architect who works with Aldo, are the same person. The second is that she was the last one to leave Camila's office on that afternoon. But be careful: neither fact necessarily indicates that Mercedes-Antonia murdered Camila. Someone could have been hiding in the hallway waiting for the last patient to leave, and then went in and killed Camila. I'm not saying that's what happened, but it could have. There's no point in running out to arrest Mercedes. We have to prove that she was the one who killed the doctor. Don't forget that the person hiding in the hallway could have been Aldo Bruno . . ."

"The two could have been working together," Welber said.

"Chief, they're lovers," Ramiro added, "and we have pictures of them leaving that building after spending the night together. They might have been accomplices."

"You're reeling from this new discovery. But what you're suggesting doesn't make sense. It would be almost like killing your wife and then signing your name. And why? To sleep with someone in your office? And why get Mercedes involved? To have an accomplice and a witness? No. It doesn't make sense to me. Unless . . ."

Espinosa looked at the children running around the square, protected by the fencing from cars and people, beneath the attentive eyes of nannies and mothers.

"Unless . . . ?" Ramiro said.

"Unless it was the other way around. Mercedes was trying to get Aldo to be a witness and an accomplice. She's much more powerful than he is. I can't see Aldo Bruno killing his own wife, but I can imagine Mercedes doing it . . . with or without his knowledge. Let's not get ahead of ourselves, we can wait until tomorrow. Nobody knows what we know. If we hadn't had that picture, we never would have learned that Mercedes and Antonia were the same person. Let's calmly think about the possibilities: Mercedes and Aldo would have had to commit the crime together, or separately. Then let's think about the motive: and there, too, we have to think about the motive for one of them acting independently, or both together. I want one of you to chat informally today with the Brunos' maid to learn about their private life. I want to know how they lived together, if they fought, if they argued . . ."

The three returned to the station, where they looked through the digital camera in search of more pictures of the couple in which Mercedes's face was clearly visible, as well as shots of her in profile. They found two particularly good ones. These were blown up and copied. It was seven at night when Espinosa left the station and went home.

It was only a geographic move. Once he was home, he

kept thinking about the discovery of Mercedes's double identity. In fact, there was no mystery: there was a surprise, but no mystery. Nobody who goes in for a preliminary visit to a therapist brings a driver's license or a passport to prove their identity. In general, a therapist would ask only for a name and a phone number. Nothing more. If the person paid cash and used a cell phone to contact the therapist, there would be nothing to prove her identity or address. Espinosa had learned these things from his personal experience, in the two years of therapy he had undergone when his marriage broke up (though back then he didn't have a cell phone). Never, though, had he heard of something like this. Mercedes must have gone to great lengths to avoid bumping into Camila socially. Certainly, the decision to become her patient was taken only after she made sure that Camila's husband never came to the office. Even so, it was incredibly daring.

The chance that Mercedes had killed Camila was greater than Espinosa had admitted in his conversation with Ramiro and Welber. She had been seen by the doormen leaving the building around seven, and Aldo got to the building at nine. So the crime was committed between six in the afternoon, when Antonia got there, and nine, when Aldo found Camila. Setting aside the possibility that a stranger had killed Camila, that left Antonia, Aldo, and Maria, the still-unknown patient. That made two women and a man, the man being her husband. Espinosa thought it was improbable that Aldo would have killed Camila and then stripped her body, or that she would have been naked when she died and that he would have left her exposed to the cops and other members of the inevitable investigation. No matter how much he'd hated his wife, Espinosa couldn't see him doing that. Besides, nothing suggested that he had hated his wife. Another idea that was growing on Espinosa was that Camila had been killed by a woman . . . and the nudity of the victim would be a message to her husband: "Look how your pretty wife took care of her patients." That hypothesis could work in the case of Mercedes, alias Antonia. Pretty, smart, and daring, she had become Aldo's mistress, turning him into an accomplice, real or imaginary, to the murder. The case would be even stronger if Mercedes-Antonia also turned out to have been Camila's lover.

Though he thought it was improbable that Aldo had killed his wife or had had anything to do with her death, his opinion had completely changed with regard to the homeless man, Elias do Nascimento. In Espinosa's mind, Aldo had killed Skinny. But something told him he'd never manage to pin either of these deaths on the architect.

He checked his freezer for his supply of frozen foods. The best he could find was spaghetti and meatballs. At least it was better than spaghetti without meatballs, he thought. There was no more wine left, but he did have two cans of beer. For dessert, the only thing he had was the diet jam he ate on his breakfast toast. There was, of course, nothing stopping him from going out, but he'd just gotten home, tired and looking forward to a nice shower before returning to his book. He went to sleep after a bad dinner, having failed to concentrate on his reading. He'd had better nights.

He awoke in the middle of the night, eyes wide open, unable to recall the dream that had woken him so abruptly. The only thing that was shining in the darkness like a neon sign was the word "many." Then he remembered "fingerprints." He turned on the light and sat up in bed. It wasn't a dream! He wasn't remembering a dream, it was his conversation with Chief Lajedo from the Leblon precinct. When Espinosa had asked him if they had found any fingerprints in Camila's office, he'd said "many."

The hypothesis that had popped into his mind before he'd fallen asleep—that Mercedes-Antonia was Camila's lover—stopped being a mere hypothesis and started to gain color and detail. He imagined Antonia's last session with Camila, moving from words to action, softly at first, with light touches of the hands, followed by Antonia gripping Camila's hand and pulling it toward her on the couch . . . minutes later, the two saying their good-byes and hugging . . . the couch too narrow for the two of them . . . Antonia moving toward the rug and pushing away the furniture— chairs and the coffee table—to give them more room. . . . And that was when . . . if the scene had played out as he imagined—and he wasn't exactly imagining it but remembering similar scenes of himself with Irene at his apartment—they would have left fingerprints on the legs of the chairs and the table . . .

After sleeping fitfully the rest of the night, he got up and thought it over again, afraid that details might have been lost in his sleep. He looked at his watch. It was not yet seven. He showered, fetched his paper from the lobby, made breakfast, and waited until he got to the station before calling his colleague.

"Lajedo, I need some information about the case of the doctor. When I asked if you had found prints, you said 'many.' Were they identified?"

"No. Two of them are from unknown persons, possibly the two patients, Maria and Antonia, that we haven't been able to find."

"Another thing. Did you find any prints on the legs of the chairs or the coffee table?"

"Funny you should ask. We found a lot from a single person: one of the two unidentified ones."

"Could you e-mail me the unidentified print, with the rest of them?"

"In one minute you'll have them all."

"Thanks."

Espinosa had no doubt about the "many" prints found on the legs of the table and chairs. His request to Lajedo was only a confirmation of what he already suspected. As soon as the images arrived, he called Aldo Bruno's office asking for Mercedes, but neither of them was there. He called Ramiro and Welber.

"Good morning, Chief."

"Morning. I'd like you to get the addresses of all the drugstores in Ipanema between the Praça Nossa Senhora da Paz and the Jardim de Alá. Then I want you to get two pictures of Aldo Bruno and two of Mercedes and come back here."

After fifteen minutes, the two were back with a printed list and file.

"Chief, we found twenty-five pharmacies in Ipanema on the Internet. We think the list is out of date, but if it's right then half of them are in the part of Ipanema you requested."

"Great. Take a cab to the last block of Ipanema and get out, each of you on one side of Rua Visconde de Pirajá, and walk until you reach the square. Take your cell phones . . . and the pictures."

"What are we looking for, Chief?"

"You are going to find out who sells flunitrazepam. The brand name is Rohypnol. If the pharmacists ask for a warrant, speak to me, but tell them that you're not trying to get the formula, you're just trying to locate a seller. It's prescription only, but the buyer could have given a false name and address. Any name will do, but the main detail to look for is when the sale took place: on the day of Camila Bruno's death, or the day before or the day before that. If any sale matches that description, show them the pictures of Mercedes and Aldo Bruno. Any news, call me."

To the officers' surprise, the drug was sold much less often than they'd suspected. At some of the pharmacies, a whole week could go by without a single sale. In the twelve pharmacies they examined, there were only four records of a sale in the days preceding Camila's murder. Of the four, three names and addresses were authentic, and only one was fake. At the pharmacy where the person gave a fake name, two salespeople had a vague idea that they had seen the man in the pictures, but neither could swear to it. Neither remembered having seen Mercedes.

Later that afternoon, Espinosa got a call from Aldo, who said he'd spoken to Mercedes. She was not in Rio, but at his request, she would come back sooner than planned, arriving the next morning.

"Who called, you or her?"

"I did."

"Did she say where she was?"

"No. When I asked, she changed the subject, and I didn't ask again."

"Did you say that I had been in the office looking for her?"

"No. It was a quick conversation. Since she said she'd be back tomorrow, I didn't worry about it . . ."

"Tell me something, sir. Did your wife and Mercedes know each other?"

"Only by name; they never met. Coincidentally, on the rare occasions when Camila came by the office, Mercedes had gone out to check on a project."

Espinosa thought it wiser not to comment. If Mercedes planned to keep her promise to come back the next day, he could clear up his doubts directly with her.

The next morning, Ramiro and Welber told Espinosa about the conversation they'd had the day before with Aldo and Camila's housekeeper. She'd been alone and had spoken freely, confirming what they had suspected: the couple had had an affectionate relationship without much friction. They'd been nice to each other and caring and attentive toward their children. There was no suggestion of a separation, even a temporary one.

"It's probable, then, that the relationship between Aldo and Mercedes was initiated by her, not him. And she has enough firepower to penetrate any fortress," Espinosa commented.

From the station, Ramiro and Welber went to wait for Mercedes's return. They still didn't know what exactly she'd done, but they had an idea of what she was capable of. The two discoveries they'd made about her were enough to hint at the desires that motivated her: she'd had a patient-therapist relationship for months with her boss's wife, using a fake name and hiding the fact of where she worked. That in itself would be enough to raise eyebrows. Not content with that, she'd initiated an amorous relationship with her boss, a relationship she'd kept up after her therapist's murder. So there was more than enough motive there to justify keeping an eye on her . . . just like she had had more than enough motive to lie low for a few days. What complicated the situation a bit was that Mercedes could now be found at three different addresses: her own apartment, the apartment her friend had loaned her, and her office. The cops decided to start with the office. That way they could keep an eye on Aldo as well as Mercedes.

Just before noon, Mercedes showed up looking exuberant,

gorgeous as ever in a low-cut dress, passing at a safe distance from the café where Welber and Ramiro were on their second or third coffee.

"She's arrived in full force," Ramiro said.

"Dressed to kill," said Welber. "Sorry, just a figure of speech."

Without glancing to the side or behind, indifferent to whether she was being watched, Mercedes entered the building and got into the elevator.

"And now, boss, what do we do?"

"Let's go back to the car and wait for her to come down, with or without Aldo . . . and then we'll follow both of them. If they go in different directions, we'll follow her. She might try to disappear again."

"And are we going to follow her twenty-four hours a day?"

"Of course not."

"So then what?"

"We're not going to do anything. She is."

"Ramiro, have you become a psychic?"

"No, but of course she'll do something. If she's guilty, she set this whole thing up planning to get Aldo and stay with him. In that case, either she gets him—that is, they move in together and eventually get married—or Aldo dumps her, and she, desperate after everything she's done for him, kills him or tries to kill him. And then we get her."

"There's just one detail, buddy. Did you inform her of the little screenplay you've written? And what if she didn't kill Camila? Your whole soap opera goes straight down the drain. Don't forget that two hours passed between her leaving the doctor's office and the discovery of the body by Aldo. Enough time for someone else to have committed the crime. Mercedes is smart. She knows that any patient or ex-patient, or even any lunatic in the building, could have killed Camila."

"And what about getting treated by Camila under an assumed name?"

"Maybe because if she said who she was Camila wouldn't have taken her as a patient."

"And why was it so important to get treated by Camila?"

"Because she really needed the help."

"Welber, you've been talking too much with Espinosa."

The last sentence was still ringing in their ears when they saw Aldo and Mercedes emerge from the building and get into a cab. They followed the car to the Rua Leopoldo Miguez. There, Aldo and Mercedes stopped in front of her friend's building and they got out of the cab holding hands.

"Let's have lunch. It's too masochistic to spend hours in this car thinking about what they're doing up there," said Ramiro.

4

Aldo felt paralyzed in all his movements, whether he was at home or at work. At any moment the doorbell could ring and Espinosa or his assistants could show up. Since they had discovered his affair with Mercedes, he inferred that he had been followed since the beginning of the investigation. The difference is that they were now doing it without even taking the trouble to hide.

Friday afternoon, after spending a few hours with Mercedes in the apartment in the Rua Leopoldo Miguez, he went out alone to head back to the office. Just as he left the building, he saw a man exiting the building across the street. He was wearing jeans and a jacket too heavy for the warm day. Obviously the garment was meant to hide the weapon he was wearing on his belt. Aldo kept walking, he on one sidewalk and the man on the other, both toward the Avenida Copacabana. When they got to the corner of the avenue, the man greeted a woman who was looking into a shop window and who remained there when the man crossed the street toward the bus stop. An obvious disguise. Aldo kept walking toward the office without checking to see if the woman had followed him—the cops had been acting so openly in the last few days that there was no real reason left for disguises or feints. At the office, he gave the interns the rest of the day off and told the doorman that he was not seeing anyone. He sat in his swivel chair and pointed it toward the sea.

What did the chief mean by telling him that the man killed in the dead-end street was called Elias do Nascimento? What kind of game was he playing with him? Why switch the man's name? To create a conflict and force him to reveal himself? If that was what he was planning, it was a clever trap: he'd been so surprised that he'd almost confessed that the man's name was Nilson, not Elias. Basic mistake. He'd stupidly fallen into the officer's trap. He'd have to be very careful with what he said. . . . The officer was skillful, skipping quickly from a question about Camila to a question about the homeless man . . .

He had to be extra careful, not only because the officer was tightening the web but also because he couldn't count on any help from Camila's family. Old Moreira da Rocha had never liked Aldo much; he thought Camila could have done much better for herself, but when their children were born and when Aldo started to enjoy professional success the old man started treating him better. Now, with his daughter dead, the old man wouldn't lift a finger to keep him from dying too. Of course he wouldn't do it himself, but Aldo was sure that he wouldn't do anything to prevent it. He and his wife would take responsibility for the grand-children. That was all they wanted.

The afternoon was clouded by a southerly wind that stirred up the sea. The panorama of the Atlantic Ocean offered views of the sun, rain, wind, waves; peaceful, light, dark, threatening, warm . . . ever since he'd rented that apartment to work in, it had never looked the same way twice. Aldo was always surprised by the constant change and the beauty of that landscape, though that afternoon he felt as gray as the clouds he was watching through the window.

He reached for a bottle of whiskey that he kept on hand in case he wanted to offer a drink to a client. In fact, he had several bottles. He took one that was already open, found a glass and some ice, and returned to his chair and his panoramic view. He didn't plan to get drunk, since he needed to remain lucid in order to face up to the officer's attack. He just wanted to relax a bit. Not too much, but just enough to think more clearly.

Thinking clearly was what he had failed to do that night in the cul-de-sac. He'd panicked and hadn't managed to remain in control of the situation. The same thing was happening now, as if Espinosa had taken the place of Nilson in his life, though the nature of the threat was entirely different. Nilson was a primeval threat, almost mythical, impossible to eliminate. . . . Yet he was in fact extinct: he'd disappeared with his death.

And now the officer had come along saying that it wasn't Nilson, it was someone named Elias. He'd known Nilson for almost forty years. . . . He knew every detail of his insane face, he knew like nobody else his gestures, his silence. . . . Who was Chief Espinosa to tell him that that wasn't Nilson?

Whatever he wanted to call him, Nilson had died in that dead-end street. Despite the darkness, the rain, and the wind, he was sure that it had been him. Just one thing he couldn't account for: the revolver.

The glass of whiskey was empty and Aldo helped himself to another shot. He was still completely master of his own mind as the day turned into night. He called home saying he would be working until a bit later . . . he would kiss his kids when he got home. The sky and the sea were black; only the streetlights illuminated the sand and the waves; the rest had disappeared into the darkness. He wanted to clear up the mystery of the vanished revolver. It was good that it was gone, but he would feel better if he knew where it had ended up. Yet it wasn't a big deal. The weapon was unregistered and the serial number had been removed. Wherever it was, it couldn't be linked to him. He was no longer looking at the world outside, but at the image of the apartment reflected in the window . . . which included his own image. His image in the window gave him food for thought, accompanied by one more shot of whiskey. After a while, he decided to move to the sofa, which was wider and more comfortable.

He woke up the next morning to the sound of the telephone ringing. It was Isabela, the nanny, wanting to know if something had happened, since the kids were asking about him. His head was throbbing and his stomach was queasy . . . he felt dizzy, he wanted to vomit, and he could hardly stand up. He'd drunk all the whiskey in the bottle, certainly more than half the total, and he hadn't had lunch or dinner the day before. He managed to get to the bathroom in time to throw up. He waited until he could pull him-self together, washed his face, left a note for Rafaela and Henrique, went downstairs, and took a taxi home.

Espinosa called in two more rookie detectives to help out Ramiro and Welber in their observations of Mercedes. The two days thereafter were tiring, if only because noth-ing else happened. Mercedes went out rarely—to the super-market and to a nearby restaurant. Their conversations with the doorman, however, turned up some news: they learned that Mercedes's residence was the same apartment on the Rua Leopoldo Miguez that she claimed she had bor-rowed from her friend. The two of them shared the apart-ment. The friend had in fact left for three months, and once Mercedes was alone she had invented the story about how she had borrowed it so that she and Aldo would have a neutral place for their rendezvous. But there weren't two apartments: it was just one, the one Espinosa's assistants were watching.

"Chief, the address where she told Aldo she lives doesn't exist. That's why she gave him her cell phone number. She's shared the apartment with a friend from college ever since graduation," Welber said over the phone.

"This girl likes disguises. I think it would be interesting for one of you to stop by the architecture school tomorrow and see what you can find. Take the pictures. See if she really is an architect. If you don't find any mention of her name, try to see if Mercedes isn't just another fake name, like Antonia."

"Chief, what if she gets suspicious and tries to leave the city?"

"Arrest her. And, Welber . . ."

"Yes, boss?"

"She doesn't know that we know about her double identity. It's important that she not find out."

"Right, boss."

As soon as he got home, Aldo stepped into the shower and let the cold water flow over his head until he felt that he'd regained the minimum of equilibrium he required to face his day. He hadn't eaten for twenty-four hours. The maid prepared him a large breakfast, while she mentioned the visit the two officers had paid and the questions they had asked.

Aldo still hadn't recovered from his hangover, and the news of the cops asking questions about his private life brought back the ghosts of the night before. Chief Espinosa was getting closer and closer. Without haste, without violence. Soon the doorbell would ring and he would appear with a search warrant for the apartment.

He finished his breakfast and went into his room. He opened and searched all the drawers in his closet and wardrobe, the shelves, Camila's boxes and purses, the pockets of their coats, the insides of suitcases and bags, underneath the bed, everything, until there was not a single place where a revolver could be hiding. The revolver was not in that room, and he was sure that neither he nor Camila would keep a firearm anywhere else in the house. The office! If he had hidden the revolver anywhere, it would have been in the office, not at home. He would go to the office at the end of the afternoon and search every inch of it. Unless he hadn't hidden it . . . if, for example, he had just thrown it into the sea. But how would he have done that? Could he have been walking down the beach at night, and when nobody was looking tossed the weapon into the surf? That would be childish, naïve, and dangerous. Anyone walking along the sidewalk could have seen a fully dressed man, at night, throwing a suspicious object into the water. He could have taken the car and thrown the weapon into the sea from the top of the Avenida Niemeyer or from the Rio-Niterói Bridge. What scared him was that he didn't have the slightest memory of having done any of those things. And if he couldn't remember, Espinosa could find the weapon before he did. He had to protect himself and his children; he couldn't let his own life and theirs be destroyed because of a random death. He had been attacked and persecuted his entire life by a useless and perverse bum. . . . Nothing more justifiable than attacking when it came to a final confrontation. That revolver, whose make he no longer even recalled, could destroy his life. He had begun to believe that the weapon had never existed, that he had never even owned one . . . which was why he couldn't remember anything about it . . . neither having thrown it away, nor what it looked like, nor having ever used it against anyone. The only thing that proved the contrary was that Nilson had shown up dead in that street the morning after their confrontation. . . . And people don't appear dead with a shot in the chest if nobody pulled the trigger.

Early in the morning, Ramiro requisitioned a car to go to the Ilha do Fundão to search for signs of Mercedes's presence at the School of Architecture. The school was located in the same building as the administration, in University City. After asking around, he learned that he should start looking in the teaching section of the university, where he could find lists of the students who had enrolled since the school was computerized. For records earlier than that, he would have to look through the filing cabinets by hand. The name he had, which Aldo had provided, was Mercedes Oliveira. The secretary was cooperative and tried all the combinations. There were a few Mercedeses and a quite a few Oliveiras, but no Mercedes Oliveira. He tried Antonia Oliveira. After other possible combinations failed to turn anything up, Ramiro showed the pictures of Mercedes to the teaching faculty, the secretaries, and the doormen. Several recognized Mercedes as Maria Antonia Castanheira. And they also remembered some stories about her. Ramiro called Espinosa.

"Boss. I've got news. Our architect isn't named Antonia or Mercedes or Oliveira, but Maria Antonia Castanheira. Several employees remembered her. I didn't speak to the professors, since some of the stories involved professors. If you want just the information, my work here is done, but if you want documents to prove it I'll have to put in a request and come back tomorrow to get them."

"These stories about professors involved affairs?"

"Yes indeed. One with a professor thirty years older, married and the father of several children . . . older than she was. The least of what happened to him was that his wife kicked him out. Two months later, Maria Antonia dumped him. He was ruined, personally and professionally."

"You said there were other stories."

"Another rather loud story involved a woman professor."

"Another affair?"

"That's right. She was also married. When Maria Antonia threatened to leave her, she tried to kill herself. She didn't succeed, but just like the male professor her professional life was ruined. I'll tell you the rest when I return."

"Good work, Ramiro, come on back. If we need any documents, we'll send for them later."

Examining the map of Ipanema, Espinosa noted that the pharmacy that had sold the sedative to the buyer with a false name and address was three blocks from Camila's office. There were other pharmacies closer by. The area around Camila's building had more pharmacies than anywhere else in the neighborhood, but the purchaser had chosen the farthest one, perhaps thinking that if there was an investigation the police would home in on the closest ones. Espinosa knew perfectly well that his reasoning was fragile, based only on his suspicion that the murderer was a nervous amateur. In fact, the drug could have been bought in another neighborhood, not necessarily shortly before the crime, or even by another person besides the criminal. The search in question was really based only on one of the chief's usual reveries, which sometimes worked out. Pleading in favor of Espinosa's suspicion was only the fact that the prescription had been issued the same day as Camila Bruno's death. He recognized that it didn't yet add up, but he kept imagining what it all meant, even if none of it would eventually add up. But that's how it always was. With time, his conjectures gained consistency and became verifiable hypotheses.

He called to schedule a meeting with Mercedes and Aldo for the end of that afternoon. Both of them tried to get out of it, but Espinosa's reasoning—that the other option would be an order to appear at the station—won the day. They arranged to meet at five in the afternoon.

At five o'clock Espinosa rang their office doorbell, accompanied by Ramiro and Welber. The door was opened by the two interns, who invited them in. Espinosa thought they seemed to have been trained to do just that. Neither seemed happy or comfortable, though not as unhappy and uncomfortable as Mercedes and Aldo when they appeared in the doorway separating the two offices.

The three cops greeted the architects. Then they all went into the conference room.

"Can we let the interns go?" Mercedes asked.

"Absolutely," Espinosa replied.

Mercedes went into the other room to tell Rafaela and Henrique that they could go home, which they did.

The three cops sat down on one side of the table, and the two architects sat on the other.

"I need to tell you that this is the last time we will meet in unofficial or semiofficial circumstances," Espinosa said. "From today on, our contacts will take place at the Twelfth Precinct, until the investigation is wrapped up. This is the last informal meeting."

"Can you, informally, tell us what we are suspected of, or what we're about to be accused of?" Aldo asked.

"Before the end of the meeting you will know."

"And if we feel pressured or intimidated by the presence of three policemen in our office, can we ask you to leave?"

"You can. But then you will have to leave as well. We will all go down to the station. Of course, at that point, you should call your lawyers."

There was a general silence that lasted a few seconds. Aldo spoke again.

"Officer, I can speak for my colleague as well as myself when I say that we understand that you have acted kindly in avoiding a police inquiry that would certainly be much more difficult for us than these meetings that you describe as informal. I think we can accept this interrogation, informally."

"Thank you. That will make it easier, though no less disagreeable."

Espinosa waited a few seconds for Aldo and Mercedes to absorb what he had just declared.

"Then we can get started by clearing up a few doubts about the identity of Mercedes . . . or Antonia . . . or Maria Antonia. What I want to know is: Which is it? Or are there others we don't know about yet?"

Mercedes's shock was as great as Aldo's.

"What's this about all these different names?" Aldo asked.

"Apparently, Mr. Bruno doesn't know about Mercedes's multiple identities, or about the multiple personalities they represent. Madam, would you be so kind as to clear up this first question?"

"They're not different identities, they're just different names for the same person. That happens often enough."

"Does it also happen often enough that people use different names to become patients of a therapist who is also their boss's wife?"

"What?!" Aldo exclaimed, rising from his chair.

"Antonia, alias Mercedes, had been a patient of Dr. Camila Bruno's for several months, without ever telling her that she knew you—nor, of course, that you were her boss and, more recently, her lover. I find it hard to believe that you, sir, didn't know about this, given the intimacy between you."

"I refuse to continue with this farce. I want to call my lawyer," said Aldo.

"In that case we can go back to the first question you asked at the beginning of the meeting: What are you suspected of? You are suspected of murder. In your case, Mr. Bruno, of two murders."

"Two murders?"

"You will probably be named as an accomplice in the murder of your wife, as well as in the murder of Elias do Nascimento . . . who, from what I can make out, you killed thinking he was someone else."

"He's not the accomplice in anything," Mercedes interrupted. "He killed Dr. Camila all by himself, without anybody's help, and he's enough of a coward to shoot down a poor sick man, half-starved and with only one leg. I didn't kill Dr. Camila . . . I loved her. We loved each other. I made up a name in order to be her patient. On that afternoon, when I left her office, she was alive and in a good mood. I was the last patient of the day. I know that because when I left there was nobody waiting in the hallway, and sometimes I would eat a sandwich in the café in the bookstore and see the doctor come in to buy a book. The building has several elevators. Aldo could have come up in one, killed his wife, then gone down and returned to discover the cadaver. He was even disgusting enough to take off her clothes to suggest that she'd had a rendezvous or was the victim of a sexual pervert . . . which she probably was."

Mercedes's tone was firm, unhesitating, and with an unmistakable edge of repugnance for what she had just said.

"Then why did you become his lover?"

"Because it was the only way to get him to tell me anything. He had almost confessed that he had killed the homeless man. . . . With a bit more time and intimacy, he would have said something about Camila's death."

"Can you describe your last session with Dr. Camila

Bruno? Not what was said, obviously, but how it went, in terms of behavior."

"What do you mean? What do you want to know?"

"I want to know where Dr. Bruno sat . . . where you sat . . . if you sat on the other chair or if you were lying on the couch . . ."

"As always, she sat in the chair and I lay on the couch."

"And then?"

"Then what?"

"After she sat down and you lay down."

"After the session was over we got up, said good-bye, and I left."

"Neither of you got up during the session?"

"Of course not."

"Sorry, Mercedes, it's just that I don't know how a session like that works."

"Well, Officer, people don't wander around or change places the whole time."

"Got it. Then can you explain to me how your fingerprints ended up on the legs of the coffee table and on the legs of the two chairs in the room? Did you by any chance decide to rearrange Dr. Bruno's office during or after the session?"

"What are you trying to say?"

"I'm trying to say that something more than a simple doctor's appointment happened in that room. . . . Perhaps even a murder."

5

Aldo and Mercedes testified at the station on different days. Espinosa interrogated them in the presence of Ramiro or Welber, who occasionally interjected. Mercedes's testimony began with a repetition of what she'd said in Aldo's office: she stated that the only thing illicit she'd done—and she stressed that it was more morally illicit than legally illicit—was to change her name.

"And I'd like to add," she said, "that from a clinical point of view it's irrelevant. There are no lies in psychoanalysis. Saying that my name is Antonia or Maria or Mercedes is clinically irrelevant. Sooner or later the question would surface in my sessions, and would be treated clinically. If you think that I changed my name with the deliberate plan of someday killing Dr. Bruno, I'm very sorry, but it's a poor rationale. I wouldn't be naïve or stupid enough to give a false name to the analyst, something that is easy enough to discover, just so that I could show up on the day and time we'd scheduled, which was certainly marked in her agenda, in order to kill her. Think about it. What do I gain from killing Dr. Bruno? Her husband? You yourselves have already seen that that wasn't necessary. To become a partner in the firm? To marry Aldo Bruno? Please, people, there are plenty of men who are better-looking, less depressive, younger, and without a murder to their credit.

As for my fingerprints on the furniture, what happened was that after the session was over I got up, ran my hand through my hair too quickly, and one of my earrings fell out. I didn't see where it fell. It's a little gold earring I brought with me from Portugal. The rug in the room is sand-colored. I couldn't see where it fell. That's when I got down to look under the furniture and moved it out of the way."

"Can you describe the earring?"

"It's a little round gold earring."

"With a screw back?"

"That's right."

"Can you explain to me how you managed, in the simple act of running your hand through your hair, to remove an earring screwed into your ear?"

"It must have been worn."

"Right. And did you find it?"

"Only after a thorough search."

"And after moving chairs and tables around."

"It was the only way."

"Was that before or after you had a drink?"

"Drink?"

"You two didn't drink anything before or after the session?"

"Officer, I didn't go to a wine tasting, I went to my analyst."

"I didn't say it was wine."

"I said wine, but I might have said whiskey or vodka. The point is, we didn't drink anything."

"Strange, because alcohol was found in the doctor's blood . . . alcohol and flunitrazepam . . . known as Rohypnol."

"I don't know what you're talking about."

Mercedes's interrogation went on for the rest of the day, with Espinosa and Ramiro taking turns. It was already dark when Mercedes confessed that her sessions with Dr. Bruno had given way to little touches on the hair and arms, and that those little touches had given way to light stroking, that the light stroking had eventually led to something more, until it had ended up as passionate, limitless sexual encounters. That had been going on for almost two months when Camila was killed. According to Mercedes, that was all that had happened between them. It was crazy to imagine that she had killed Camila.

Aldo Bruno's deposition was almost entirely conducted by Espinosa; Ramiro and Welber interrupted only to clarify the architect's replies. The small room contained no more than a table and two chairs, one facing the other, with two more along the wall, where Ramiro and Welber sat.

"Mr. Bruno, do you feel ready to go ahead with this interview, which in fact we began at your office?" Espinosa began.

"And to finish it as quickly as possible."

"Can you tell us one more time at what time you arrived at Dr. Bruno's office building on the day of her death?"

"At nine o'clock."

"How long did you stay there?"

"It's very hard to say. What I found there completely shocked me. . . . It might have been five minutes, it might have been half an hour. It's impossible to say."

"Was that the only time that day you were in her office?"

"Yes. When the police arrived, I didn't want to go back in. . . . I waited outside . . . then the officer . . . I don't remember his name . . . asked me a series of questions."

"Lajedo is his name."

"Sorry, but I don't remember."

"And before you found the body?"

"What do you mean?"

"You weren't there at any time before you found the body?"

"No. Before, I was home with my children. I only went to the office after I called to see what was taking Camila so long, since she was always home by eight. I called the office and her cell phone. Nobody answered. I started to worry and went over there. . . . But I've already told you this more than once, sir."

"Sorry, we just need to eliminate some of the remaining doubts."

"What doubts?"

"Little details . . . we're getting there. When you opened the door of Dr. Bruno's office, what was it that shocked you most at first? The fact that she was naked or the evidence that she was dead?"

"I . . . It's hard to say. . . . I don't know . . ."

"Or could it be that it was neither of those facts?"

"What exactly do you mean?"

"Exactly what I'm saying."

"What would have shocked me most at first. . . . What could shock me more?"

"Maybe you weren't shocked . . ."

"What . . ."

". . . because of the simple fact that you had seen that scene two hours before."

"You're crazy, Officer. What leads you to believe that?"

"Listen to the little story I'll tell you. If it's crazy, we'll leave it there. . . . It goes like this: you discovered— I don't know how, and that's one of the doubts I still have—that Dr. Bruno had a few little eccentricities in her clinical practice . . . such as having sexual relations with some of her female patients . . . relations marked by intense passion—"

"Don't insult my wife, Officer!"

"I'm not, sir. I have no judgment about her behavior; I'm just trying to sketch out something that for me is still a bit hazy. But please, let me finish my story. As I was saying, you made this discovery . . . I'm not sure if it was accidental, in a surprise visit to her office, or if someone told you about it. In the first case, you wouldn't need any further proof. If you had been told about it, you might have tried to discover what was going on. The fact is, however it happened, that you figured it out. That was probably when, perhaps in a reaction to the discovery, you started your affair with Mercedes. I don't know how much she contributed toward the mortal hatred you developed for Dr. Bruno, your wife, the mother of the children you loved, who was suddenly transformed into someone sexually perverse, displaying degrading behavior that could become public, which would hurt the reputation of your children . . . et cetera, et cetera. That was when you decided to put an end to the story, probably with the contribution of a bit of extra pushing."

Aldo Bruno was sweating abundantly. He searched in his pockets for a handkerchief with which to wipe his face, but didn't find one. Welber found some tissues in the next room and placed the box on the table, in front of him.

"Nobody . . . nobody . . ."

"By extra pushing I'm not referring to Mercedes, but to the murder of the homeless man you know as Nilson . . . You know how it is, one murder leads to another . . ."

"There's nothing . . ."

"You were already emotionally weakened by having killed the man, Nilson or Elias, the name doesn't matter . . ."

"I didn't kill him! He killed me!"

"But that's not the crime we're discussing here. We'll get there in due course. Let's return to the murder of Dr. Bruno. Once you decided to kill her, the question became *how* to kill her. We can agree that you don't have too much experience in these matters, but the objective conditions facilitated your planning. The most obvious choice was to kill her and make it look like it was the work of some patient who was a sexual maniac . . . a psychopath . . . a psychotic . . . someone quite different from the way people imagine you to be. The first time she came home and left her schedule out, you copied down the names and the times of her appointments. And waited. On that Tuesday, you left the office a bit earlier, stopped by the local store where you usually bought your clothes, bought something you needed, and went to Camila's office building, arriving a bit before seven. You entered through the garage, went up in the service elevator, and waited, hidden in the hallway, until the last patient left. The Rohypnol tablets were already crushed in your pocket, waiting to be distributed in the drink you brought along . . . maybe half a bottle of the doctor's favorite. The name of the day's last patient was Antonia. You'd seen that in her agenda. What you didn't even notice, probably due to your nervousness, was that the Antonia who left the office was none other than Mercedes, your coworker. You waited until you heard the elevator door close, emerged from your hiding place, opened the office door, and. . . . It was so easy that you were surprised. . . . A drink to commemorate something, the sedative mixed into the drink . . . and in less than twenty minutes your wife was a victim incapable of reacting or of feeling any pain. They say it's easy to kill someone but it's hard to get rid of the body. You needed to figure that one out. . . . You elected to expose the body. A clean murder, bloodless, no struggle, no weapon . . . and cowardly. After all that, you exited through the garage, went home, spent an hour playing with the kids, and started worrying that your wife wasn't home in time for dinner. . . . You called the office and her cell phone . . . and went back to the office to find the body. It might not have been exactly that, there might be a few details that don't match, but I would think that my story basically gets the gist of it."

Halfway through the story, the architect had gone completely silent and motionless. When Espinosa finished, Aldo Bruno was looking at his hands, crossed on the table, pale, the color drained from his lips and his face utterly without expression. He turned his head to the side and vomited. He threw up twice more, and while his mouth and his cheek were still dirty, before they could clean up the mess, he began a kind of monologue of jumbled, senseless phrases. His tone of voice became sharper and sharper, he started to shout words, looking straight at Espinosa, who looked questioningly at Welber and Ramiro, though none of them could make out a thing he was saying. The testimony was interrupted for half an hour, the floor was wiped up, and, in spite of the acrid smell that remained in the little room, they tried to start again . . . in vain. Even outside the room, Aldo had continued to scream insults, now at Mercedes. Back in the room, he sat in the same chair, facing Espinosa, spitting on the ground and wiping off his mouth, which was still stained by vomit. He got up and sat back down several times, to no apparent end. Eventually his physical agitation gave way to a kind of torpor occasionally punctuated by mumbling that the three cops, even with great effort, failed to understand. Then he seemed exhausted, laid his head on his crossed arms, and gave off no further sound. He was picked up by an ambulance and taken to a psychiatric hospital.

The doctors thought that it was a passing phase, a psychosis derived from an extremely traumatic situation. That is what Espinosa retained from his conversation with them. They thought that he'd recover soon enough, but a month passed without news, though the hospital had promised to inform Espinosa when Aldo was ready to be released.

He didn't plan to charge him with the murder of his wife, but with the murder of the homeless man. In fact, the investigation into Camila's death had never been under his jurisdiction. The crime had occurred outside his bailiwick. The material and the information he'd gathered about Camila Bruno had been sent on to Lajedo, in the Fourteenth Precinct, where the crime had taken place. Once his investigation was wrapped up, he still hadn't proved anything about Mercedes's involvement in Camila's murder. The public prosecutors didn't feel that they had enough on her, and even the signs of her indirect participation were not considered adequate to prosecute her.

Espinosa still wondered how Aldo had learned about his wife's sexual behavior. He thought he had probably been tipped off anonymously, and suspected Mercedes. He also suspected that Mercedes and Antonia were almost two different people. One, the sensual patient and Camila's lover; the other, an architect, a coworker and Aldo Bruno's lover. Two separate worlds. Espinosa thought, moreover, that she was perverse enough to be able to deal quite well with the duality, and to obtain twice the advantages, not to mention twice the pleasure, from the situation.

The murder of the homeless man Elias do Nascimento was different. It hadn't occurred in someone else's jurisdiction, but only a few feet from Espinosa's station, and he was convinced that Aldo Bruno had fired his revolver in the middle of that storm thinking it was Nilson . . . if such a person had ever really existed.

Camila's murder was out of his range; however, Elias had been killed underneath his nose. Espinosa thought it was likely that Aldo would someday understand what had really happened on that dead-end street. But Espinosa wasn't a shrink, he wasn't interested in Aldo Bruno's personal disturbances. He was interested in the fact that he'd murdered two people.

A week later, the hospital called to say that Aldo Bruno would be released the next morning.

At eight o'clock on a pretty late-summer morning, Espinosa and Welber were waiting for Aldo in the hospital lobby, but he had hanged himself in the night.